HARLEQUIN™

Western

A BULL RIDER TO DEPEND ON

JEANNIE WATT

HARLEQUIN®

Western Romance

Romance—the Western way!

AVAILABLE THIS MONTH

ISBN-13: 978-0-373-75756-5

EAN

HWESTATMIFC0417

"You never answered my question," Tyler said.

Skye tipped her chin up. "What question is that?" she asked, knowing full well what he was referring to.

"The one about why we never got along."

She gave a careless shrug. "I don't know... Spiders. Snakes. The incessant teasing?" His knack for finding little weaknesses and insecurities and exploiting them. "You were merciless toward me."

"You mean I was acting like a preadolescent boy who liked a girl?"

She stared at him, stunned, as heat flooded her cheeks, which was ridiculous.

Tyler gave a little laugh. "You didn't know?"

"How could I know?"

"I thought I was telegraphing my feelings pretty well back then."

Skye rolled her eyes, thankful to have something to distract her from the other questions crowding into her head—such as why had he asked her out in high school?

He hooked his thumb into his belt loop. "This isn't going to be easy, is it?"

"I see no way that it can be." Skye spoke truthfully, thankful that he hadn't clued in to the direction of her thoughts.

Dear Reader,

Who doesn't love a bad boy?

Why, that would be my heroine, Skye Larkin. Recently widowed, she's all about predictability and security. Her friend Jess Hayward is the poster child for predictable, responsible behavior, but his bull-riding twin, Tyler...not so much. Unfortunately, Tyler is the one with the resources to help her out of her financial jam.

Tyler has had a crush on Skye forever, but Skye has never wanted anything to do with him or his wild ways. So how to convince her that he's every bit as dependable as his brother? That's Tyler's dilemma, and that was what made this book so much fun to write.

I love writing my bull-riding heroes and describing their journeys as they find their perfect women. Now that I've finished Tyler's story, and those of his bull-riding buddies Trace Delaney and Grady Owen, I'm embarking on the story of his twin brother, Jess, who will also hit some bumps along the road to happiness. Imagine that. ☺

Best wishes and happy reading,

Jeannie Watt

A BULL RIDER
TO DEPEND ON

JEANNIE WATT

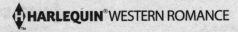
HARLEQUIN® WESTERN ROMANCE

Recycling programs
for this product may
not exist in your area.

ISBN-13: 978-0-373-75756-5

A Bull Rider to Depend On

Printed in U.S.A.

Jeannie Watt makes her home in Montana's beautiful Madison valley, where she and her husband raise heritage beef. When she's not writing, Jeannie enjoys collecting patterns and sewing vintage clothing, riding in the mountains and hiking with her husband. Sometimes she goes fishing, too, but she usually daydreams more than she fishes.

Books by Jeannie Watt

Harlequin Western Romance

Montana Bull Riders

The Bull Rider Meets His Match
The Bull Rider's Homecoming

Harlequin Superromance

The Brodys of Lightning Creek

To Tempt a Cowgirl
To Kiss a Cowgirl
To Court a Cowgirl
Molly's Mr. Wrong

The Montana Way

Once a Champion
Cowgirl in High Heels
All for a Cowboy

Visit the Author Profile page
at Harlequin.com for more titles.

To Gary—the man with whom I've somehow managed to spend every major holiday without electricity.

Chapter One

Skye Larkin hated thinking ill of the dead, but as she pushed through the bank doors for the fourth time in two weeks, she was very, very angry with her late husband. And beyond being angry, she was, for the first time since learning the true state of her finances, afraid.

It'd been a shock, yes, to discover that the money she thought she had socked away to see the ranch through lean times was no longer there—that her husband had drained the accounts during his road trips, despite his assurances that he'd given up gambling—but for the first six months after Mason has passed away, she'd told herself it would be all right. She'd squeak through somehow. Make the payments, start to pull ahead.

At the six-month mark she had to face the reality that she wasn't pulling ahead. In fact, after a couple of disasters, she was falling further behind, and the money she'd counted on to see her through these rough spells was now in the coffers of some high-rise Vegas casino.

Damn Mason's gambling.

And not to mention all of his buddies who encouraged him to go out when he shouldn't have. If Mason had stayed in his hotel room as he wanted—as he'd promised—then he wouldn't have gambled. But no. His buddies would have none of that. One buddy in particular. And Mason had never been one to say no to a friend—even if that friend was nudging him along on the path to self-destruction.

Skye's mouth tightened as she jerked open the truck door. She was behind one payment on the ranch and two payments on the truck. The first of the month—payment time—was inching closer, and she was rapidly running out of options. She climbed inside and rested her forehead on the steering.

She couldn't operate the ranch without the yearly cow loan—the money that saw her through until she sold cattle. Having very few paydays during the year was the reason for the ranch account. Mason had no doubt planned to pay the account back with his next big win, either in the bull-riding arena or at the tables.

Mason always had big plans and every intention of carrying them out. He was young and no doubt thought he'd have lots of time to accomplish what he wanted, to rebuild Skye's small family ranch, to start breeding bulls. An inattentive driver on the Vegas strip had put an end to all of that. And an end to Skye's inherent belief that everything would work out if she was patient enough.

Things were nowhere close to working out.

Skye pressed her lips together and put the truck in gear. The now-familiar grinding sound came from the rear as she backed up, but, as usual, it disappeared when she put the truck in a forward gear. She ignored it. Worrying wouldn't help anything. If it did, then the ranch would be solvent.

And now, plan B. The one she'd hoped to avoid. But after Mason's funeral, her friend Jess Hayward had told her to call if she needed help. Made her promise to call. And she was going to make that call, regardless of whom he was related to. Now. Before she talked herself out of it.

Pulling over to the side of the road, Skye searched through her contacts and found Jess's number. As luck would have it, he was in town. That was a good sign. Right?

"Sure," he said when she asked if he had a few minutes to meet. "I'll buy you a meal."

"No, thank you." She wouldn't be able to eat while she was all worked up. "But I'll have a Coke while you eat."

"Maybe we can both have a Coke at the Shamrock and you can tell me what's up."

"Yes. That sounds good." Ten minutes later she walked in the door of Gavin, Montana's favorite drinking establishment and crossed the room to where Jess was already waiting at a table with two large Cokes in front of him.

Skye sat down and attempted a casual smile, which was harder than it should have been, due to the butterflies battling it out in her midsection. "It's been a while."

"Yeah. It has." There was a touch of irony in his voice. Well deserved, since it had been over six months since she'd seen him.

"I'm sorry about that. Work and the ranch." She made a small gesture. "You know."

The expression in his eyes told her he understood

what she was trying to say. She'd holed up physically as well as emotionally.

"This is really hard, Jess, so I'm just going to spit it out. Would you be able to float me a loan? Short term?"

"How much?" He made a move for his wallet, and Skye put up a hand, stopping him.

"A lot." She took a steadying breath. "I'm behind on the truck payments. It's close to paid off, and I don't want it to go back to the bank."

Jess's expression clouded, and Skye continued before she lost her nerve. "I'm a little behind on the ranch, too."

"Wow, Skye." He spoke softly.

"Not a lot there. One payment, and I'm going to make a double payment this month and catch up. But those two things together have made it so that I can't get a cow loan. And if I can't get a cow loan, then I can't operate, and what I make at the day job is a pittance compared to what I need." She leaned back, feeling drained after the blurted confession. "I should have never agreed to mortgage the place, but obviously, I hadn't expected Mason to die."

Jess shifted in his chair. "I'm not in a good place right now."

"Oh. I thought…" Skye's voice trailed off. Rumor had it that when Jess's parents sold the family ranch, they'd given each of their twin sons a healthy portion of the profits. If it hadn't been for that much-repeated story, she would never have asked. "I apologize."

"No." He looked affronted. "I know why you asked, but Ty and I pretty much insisted that the folks invest the profit from the ranch into their own futures." One corner of his mouth tightened a little. "They didn't make a lot of money on the sale. Just enough to get out from under the debt and get started again in Texas."

"That's what I get for listening to rumors," Skye said, still feeling embarrassed. "According to some of the old boys, you and Ty are rolling in dough."

"That's why I'm living in a crappy camp trailer."

Skye started to smile in spite of herself. "I guess I should tell you that rumor has it you're just biding your time until you start building your 'big house.' You're in the process of looking for the right piece of property."

Jess laughed and then reached for his untouched drink. Skye did the same. She still had the problems she had when she walked in, but somehow, talking to Jess made her feel better. As if she weren't all alone.

"You know, Skye..." She looked up from her glass in time to see an uncertain expression play across his features. "Tyler's doing well. He's had a couple big paydays. The last one was huge."

It felt as if a barrier had slammed into place at the sound of his twin's name. "And I'm certain he wants to share his money with me. If I talked to him, he'd probably loan you the money."

"Can't do it," Skye said. Because Tyler Hayward had been a big part of Mason's problem and she didn't see how she could live with herself if she tried to make him part of the solution.

Jess didn't try to argue with her. He knew better. When they'd been kids growing up within a few miles of one another, she and Jess had become good friends. His twin, not so much. Tyler had been brash and loud and kind of mean. To her anyway. Snakes, spiders, smart-aleck remarks. He'd never shown any mercy.

Childhood issues she could have forgiven, but he'd

also been instrumental in causing her current situation—*that* she couldn't forgive. Tyler and Mason had been good friends. Great friends—the kind who gambled and drank together. Mason had tried so hard to give up the gambling, but, as he'd told her so often, the only way he could do that was to not go out. Tyler Hayward was all about the party, and he wanted his good buddy with him. The thing that really got to her was that she'd specifically asked Tyler to stop encouraging Mason to go out, and he'd blatantly ignored that request, which was why she wasn't about to humble herself before him now and ask for money. She'd find a way.

"I assume you've had no luck with the banks."

Skye shook her head. "Not for lack of trying. I owe too much on the mortgage to use the place as collateral. If I can get the cow loan, catch up on the truck… I think I'll be okay. I'll have to live really tightly for a year or two…" Her voice trailed off as she watched the expression shifting on Jess's face. This was killing him almost as much as it was killing her. "But hey," she said, forcing a smile that didn't fool either of them. "I've been through worse. You know I have."

Jess let out a breath. "If it's okay, I'll make some inquiries—no names—just to see if anyone can float a cow loan."

"I'd appreciate it," Skye said softly.

"I know how hard it is for you to ask."

Indeed, Skye was not a good asker—not after having self-sufficiency hammered into her for her entire life.

"That's why I came to you," Skye said. "You get it." Unlike his brother. Why couldn't he have understood Mason's problem? Played ball? If he had...well, she couldn't say Mason would be alive today, because he'd been on his way to the casino resort to check into a room when he got hit, but she'd be a lot better off.

"And now that I know how Ty's doing with his bull riding, how are you doing with yours?"

"Stalled out at the moment. I'm living lean, still doing contract construction and trying to save enough money to follow Ty onto the circuit. You know, while I'm still young enough to get beat into the ground and bounce back."

"You're good, Jess. You should give it a shot."

He lowered his gaze to study the table, as if this wasn't a topic he was comfortable with. When he looked up at her, his expression was serious. "If I had the money, you know I'd give it to you."

"Loan it to me."

"That's what I meant. Right now, living in the camp trailer, sharing it with Ty when he's back in town...the prospect of hitting the road next year is one of the only things keeping me sane."

SKYE DROVE HOME telling herself not to worry. She still had options, and she'd worked extra shifts to catch up on the ranch loan. She just needed to do the same with the truck. And the cow loan...she'd figure something out.

The porch squeaked under her feet as she mounted the stairs—a noise she'd long equated with her husband coming home from a bull-riding event, or back from the barn after chores. A good noise still, even though it made her feel lonely. She and Mason had had good times.

She pulled out her keys and unlocked the door, holding it open so that Jinx could shoot out as usual. The big gray cat disappeared into the lilac bushes without so much as a backward glance, but come morning, after he'd done his best to decimate the mouse population in the sheds and barns, he'd be back, wanting attention and lots of it.

Skye walked inside and hung her purse on the coat rack near the door. Her house was spotless. When she couldn't sleep, she cleaned. And cleaned and cleaned. It cost very little money to clean a house, and it wore her out and thus made it possible to get at least a few hours of rest before heading to work in the morning.

But tonight she hoped she could simply fall asleep the way she used to be able to. Mason had once teased her that when ten o'clock came around, her eyes automatically shut regardless of where she was. It was for the most part true. Skye was a morning person, which was why the morning shift at the café had seemed so perfect—right up until sleep started to escape her, around the same time that the bills started stacking up.

Partial payment was now the name of the game. She hadn't been turned over to collection, but if she missed one more truck payment…

Her stomach tightened, and she hugged her arms around herself. Looked like another night of heavy cleaning and organizing.

Chapter Two

"Good thing I'm a minimalist," Tyler Hayward muttered as he edged past his brother as he made his way down the hall of the camp trailer.

"You're welcome for the roof over your head," Jess muttered back as he headed into the cramped living room.

"I appreciate it," Ty said. Cramped or not, he did.

Not that long ago, when he came home, Tyler crashed in his own room in the house he grew up in, but after his parents had sold the ranch and moved to Texas to be closer to his grandparents, he started staying with his twin. Practically on top of him, actually since his "room" was a built-in bunk in a niche in the hallway leading to Jess's small bedroom at the rear of the trailer. His gear was stacked in a pile in the living room. He had to admit that Jess was being a good sport about him invading his space. At this point in his life, he had no idea where he would eventually land, or even what state he would call home. Texas, to be close to the folks? Or Montana to be close to his twin and the people he'd grown up with? Since his parents seemed to visit Gavin every couple of months, he was leaning toward Montana, which meant getting his own place.

And for the first time ever, he was in a position to do it. His previous season had been good. No. Make that great, and he wanted to get something nailed down, pay cash and then only have to worry about maintenance and upkeep. A small place with ten acres or so. Enough to keep a few horses, a few cows. Nothing fancy.

After stowing his duffel under the bunk—at least there was room for that—he came back out into the living room/kitchen, where his brother was now settled in the living room, beer in one hand, remote in the other.

"You know…if you wanted to invest in a bigger trailer, I'd go halves with you." He'd offer more, but his brother was proud. A little too proud sometimes.

"This'll do for now."

Jess had always been the careful twin—except in the arena. Once atop a bull, he rode with the best of them. The only problem was that he was never able to commit himself to a season. To take that risk.

"One of us has to have a job," he'd say whenever Tyler badgered him to go pro. Ironically, Tyler was now the one with the money. No house, but money. Thankfully one was rather easily parlayed into the other.

"How long are you going to save?" Tyler asked as he got a beer out of the tiny fridge and joined his brother on the beat-up sofa their mom had left behind during the big move. He propped his foot up on the wooden chest that served as a coffee table.

"Before…?"

"You make some kind of a move?"

Jess changed the channel. A couple of times. "Until I feel ready. Okay?"

Tyler put up a hand. "Just checking." Again.

Jess changed channels Again. Ty figured it would be

another night of watching five minutes of a show then moving on as his brother became restless, but instead he muted the television and put the remote on his lap. "Skye came to see me today."

Ty had years of practice not reacting to Skye's name when it came up. He'd had a raging crush on her for as long as he could remember. She'd hated him for as long as he could remember. No matter what he did to impress her, it didn't work, and eventually he'd given up and decided he really didn't like her all that much anyway.

But he did. When they'd gone to high school, he'd even asked her out once. She'd thought he was poking fun at her and never gave him a chance to explain. Off to college she went, and when she came back, she was engaged to Mason. Ty's friend. A guy he liked just fine, but sometimes had a hard time respecting. Being around the newly engaged couple had been Ty's own private hell.

He knew for a fact that Mason never would have asked Skye out in the first place if he hadn't known that Tyler had a thing for her. Mason and Tyler had competed in all venues of life, and in this case, Mason had won. Skye had refused to give Tyler a chance, and that had always stung a little.

Tyler put his feet up on the trunk in front of him. "Why did Skye come to see you?"

"She needed a loan. She's behind on some payments and can't nail down a cow loan."

"How much behind?"

"I didn't get a dollar amount. She needs the cow loan." Jess raised his eyes to meet his brother's.

"I can lend her the money." He spoke flatly, as if he had no emotional stake in the matter.

"Yeah," Jess said. "I mentioned the possibility and…" He gave his head a small shake. "She wasn't in favor."

"But you're telling me anyway." He knew his brother wasn't twisting the knife, so…

"I thought you'd want to know."

"Why?"

Jess lifted an eyebrow, and Tyler let out a breath as he dropped his gaze to study the toes of his dusty boots. The thing about being a twin was that it was pretty hard to keep the guy who looked like you from reading you. He'd denied having any kind of lingering feelings for Skye after she'd married Mason—had said that he'd moved on from that hopeless affair—but Jess wasn't fooled. Ty knew because he could read his twin as easily as his twin read him.

"Right," he muttered. The situation between him and Skye was complicated—or at least it was on his end, where feelings of guilt, frustration and resentment were coupled with an attraction that refused to die. On her end, it was simple—he was the bad guy who'd encouraged her husband onto the path of self-destruction, and she'd made no secret of her beliefs.

He was guilty to a degree. Despite Skye asking him to stay far away from Mason while on tour, he hadn't seen where a few wild nights would hurt anyone—but he also hadn't known how far Mason would take the whole partying thing. By the time Tyler realized what was happening, it was too late to do anything about it. The most unfortunate part was that there wasn't a good way for Tyler to defend himself. How did you tell a woman that she didn't know everything about her husband and his code of ethics?

You didn't. Not after that guy was dead.

Jess cleared his throat. "Skye won't be happy about me telling you, but I thought...you know."

Tyler shot his brother a quick look, read the concern on his face and wondered if it was for him or Skye. He couldn't help but smirk as he said, "That she might be desperate enough to accept help from the bad twin?"

"Something like that." Jess picked up the remote and changed the channel again. "It might give you a chance to smooth things with her."

Tyler gave a *yeah, right* snort as the pitcher on the screen threw a perfect strike. "She doesn't want them smoothed."

"She doesn't know the facts."

Nor would she...although he had to admit that this might be an opportunity to show Skye that he wasn't the jerk she thought he was. He might have had difficulties controlling his wilder impulses back in the day, but beneath it all, he was a decent guy. Just like his twin.

And as far as Mason was concerned—Mason was always his own boss and Skye needed to accept that.

WHEN SKYE GOT off shift at one thirty, Jess Hayward was waiting for her by her car.

Only it wasn't Jess.

The warm smile on her face cooled as she realized that the guy loitering at the edge of the parking lot was Tyler Hayward. With the exception of the small scar on Tyler's chin, the brothers were nearly identical, right down to their haircuts—but there was something different about the way they stood. And moved. Skye had learned long ago to tell them apart at a distance. If Jess was walking toward her, she went to meet him. If it had been Tyler…she'd changed direction to avoid whatever irritating thing he was about to do to her. When they were younger, he'd threatened her with various amphibians. As they'd grown older, frogs and salamanders had changed into smart-ass comments.

"Good morning," he said as she stopped several feet away from him.

"Good morning," she echoed coolly, knowing instantly that Jess had ratted her out. With the best of intentions, no doubt, but now she had to deal with Tyler.

"You're looking good, Skye."

A compliment. That was different.

"You, too." She spoke with polite indifference, but, infuriatingly, the fact of the matter was that he really did look good.

He shifted his weight and folded his arms over his chest, as if debating how to launch into what he'd come to say. "We haven't talked in a while, Skye."

That was true. With the exception of him offering stiff condolences at Mason's funeral, they hadn't spoken since they'd faced off in the parking lot behind the Shamrock Bar almost two years ago, shortly after she'd discovered that Mason had been gambling again. She'd asked Tyler to stop encouraging her husband to go out. He'd told her he would. He'd lied.

Skye got her keys out of her pocket. No longer smiling, she tilted her head. Waited.

Tyler took the plunge. "Jess told me that you are in need of a loan."

She shook her head. "Not any longer."

"Ah." He looked as if he wanted to ask why, but her stony expression must have made him think twice.

"Thank you for asking." She hoped that would cause him to move along, and indeed he did take a couple of steps, but toward her rather than toward his truck.

"You know…" he said, his expression becoming serious. Too serious, really. "…we've had our differences, but I was Mason's friend—"

"That was the problem, wasn't it?" The angry reply burst out of nowhere, and Skye instantly clamped her mouth shut to keep from saying more. She needed to get out of there, away from this guy who so easily triggered her. She moved around him to her car, but before she could open the door, he put his hand on it. Her gaze jerked up, and he dropped his hand.

"Mason was a grown man, Skye. He made his own choices." His voice was so low and intense that it was little more than a growl.

And you didn't help matters. The words teetered on her lips, but she bit them back. She wasn't getting into this. Not here. Not now. She forced her expression to go blank and uttered a lie. "I'm sorry, Tyler. That was uncalled for." His gaze narrowed, telling her he wasn't buying the false apology. "It was a busy shift, and I'm a little tired. I didn't sleep well." Total truth, there. "I appreciate your trying to help."

"The offer stands." The way he spoke made her wonder why.

"I'll keep it in mind."

And she'd file it under Fat Chance. She was not asking for help from the man who was in a large way responsible for the situation she was now in. The very fact that he offered…

"I need to go, Ty." *Before I tell you what I'm really thinking.*

He studied her, as if debating whether or not to prolong the conversation, and she in return studied him, her gaze unwavering. He was handsome. Dark and lean and dangerous looking. Ty had always kind of intimidated her. He was so different from his easy-going twin, who'd been one of her best buddies growing up. Funny how those things went.

His mouth tightened a little as they silently regarded one another, the atmosphere growing more charged by the second, and for some reason the movement of his lips caused a tiny ripple in her midsection.

Yes. Dangerous.

Skye tore her gaze away and opened the car door. When she closed it, a wave of relief washed over her.

Safe.

Oh yeah. That had gone well.

Ty forced his tight jaw muscles to relax as he walked back to his truck while Skye all but laid rubber in her hurry to get away from him. It was obviously easier for her to blame him rather than Mason for the trouble she was in. He understood, but that didn't mean he had to like it.

Nope. He pretty much hated it. But what could he do? Chase her down and tell her the truth about her husband? He might be angry, but he wasn't that angry. He needed to let this go, focus on the here and now, on the things he could control, like where he lived.

Instead of getting into his truck, he reversed course and walked into the café.

"Hey, Ty."

Angie Salinas greeted him with a wide smile. *See, Skye... Angie likes me.* And Angie probably had more of a reason to dislike him, because they'd dated in junior high for almost a week, before he broke up with her on Valentine's Day. He was a smooth operator back then.

"Angie." He smiled up at her as she waved him to a booth. "I don't need a menu."

"Know what you want, eh?"

"Grilled chicken."

"Sandwich?"

"Just the chicken, but go ahead and charge me for a sandwich." He ate all the protein he could to keep his muscles in shape, stayed away from useless carbs. As he'd gotten older, he'd started paying more attention to things like diet and exercise. Funny how a body could get beat around for only so long before it started requiring extra attention.

"Salad or something?"

"A salad would be good. Dressing on the side."

"You got it." She jotted a few words on her pad and headed off to the counter.

Ty drank some water, did his best to tamp down the irritation still lingering after his encounter with Skye, then pulled out his phone and went to the real estate listings. He and Jess might have been wombmates who could practically read each other's minds, but if they had to share that tiny trailer space for much longer...well...he saw no good coming of that. It was time to move out.

A house would be nice, but he had nothing against buying a used trailer, as Jess had done. In the beginning anyway. The important thing was that he wanted to buy whatever he decided on and own it free and clear while he had the bucks to do so. Traveling the circuit was expensive. Keeping his bare-bones insurance policy was expensive.

When Angie brought his food, he put his phone aside. "I'm looking to buy some land," he said. "Know of anything?"

Because if anyone was going to know anything, it was Angie. She had six siblings and she worked in a café.

She cocked a hip, frowning a little as she thought. "Nothing springs to mind, but if I hear of anything I'll let you know. If you're around." One corner of her mouth quirked up. "Will you be around?"

"I'm not retiring, if that's what you mean. I'm just planning for the future."

"That is so out of character, Ty."

He grinned at her and she smiled back before heading to another table. It really wasn't out of character, but Jess was so responsible that by contrast he appeared to be reckless. He had his moments, but deep down, he wasn't all that different from his brother.

Try telling Skye that.

He wasn't going to tell Skye anything. Why beat his head on a wall?

Chapter Three

As soon as she got home, Skye took off her uniform and put it directly into the washer before pulling on worn jeans and a crewneck sweatshirt, dressing in quick jerky movements. She wanted to stop thinking—to turn off her brain and just…be.

As if.

It was going to be another sleepless night. She was certain of that, just as she was certain that Tyler was to blame…although it wasn't in the way that she usually blamed him. He'd simply uttered a truth that she hadn't wanted to hear. A truth that had echoed through her brain for the entire trip home.

Mason was a grown man. Mason had made his own choices.

She knew that. But he'd also had an addiction that his friends could have helped him manage. They didn't. End of story.

She gathered her hair into a ponytail, slapped on a ball cap and headed out the door to take care of her menagerie.

Skye loved animals, as had Mason, which was why she now had so many mouths to feed in addition to the cattle. Cattle she wouldn't have for much longer if she couldn't secure a loan to buy the hay she needed to feed them. If she had to sell the cattle at a loss, see all of her hard work go by the wayside, it was going to kill her. She could catch up on the truck payment if she sold, but without that cow money being there when she needed it, she couldn't afford the ranch. And if she couldn't afford the ranch, then she was going to have to give up her livestock.

Her animals had been the one thing that had seen her through after Mason had died. How could she even think about giving them up?

Simple. She couldn't. And she wouldn't.

Her mini-donkey, Chester, came trotting across the pasture with the old mule, Babe, not too far behind as Skye walked the short distance down the driveway to the barn. Chester ducked under the bottom wire of the fence as if it wasn't there and continued on to Skye, stopping directly in front of her. Skye reached out to rub his wiry forelock, shaking her head as Babe gave a loud protest from the pasture.

"You know it upsets him when you do this," Skye chided the little donkey, who rubbed his head on her hip, almost knocking her over. Babe called to his buddy again in his rusty voice, and Skye gave the little donkey a push. "Back to the pasture."

The donkey showed no signs of minding, so Skye went to the dwindling haystack and tossed several flakes of alfalfa over the fence into the low feeders. Chester shoved his way back under the wire and joined his friend, who was already tossing hay in the air, looking for the good stuff. Vanessa, the Canada goose she'd rescued from the creek when she'd been a hatchling, waddled out of the barn and into the pasture where Skye's mare, Pepper, and Mason's gelding, Buzz, grazed near Mr. Joe, the horse who'd raised her. The grass was tall and would feed the three for several weeks. The cows had decent pasture, too, on the remnants of the newly cut alfalfa field. Her closest neighbor, Cliff, had cut her hay twice this year... Thank goodness for good neighbors. But the fields hadn't produced nearly enough to see her through the winter.

Hay. Money. Problems.

She had one more bank appointment. A smaller bank that was friendly toward ranchers—probably the first place she should have gone, except that it was in a small town thirty miles away from Gavin, and she felt a loyalty to the bank that had given her the mortgage. The bank that was not one bit interested in working with her now that she'd hit a bump in the road.

She understood the concern, but it wasn't like she wanted the money for a vacation or something. She wanted the money so that she could make money to pay back the bank and thus save them both a lot of headaches and hassle. The bank guy didn't see it that way.

She felt hopeful about the new bank, though. She'd gone to school with the loan officer and felt certain she could talk to him as a person, explain the run of bad luck and exactly how she planned to work her way through it. One loan. That was all she needed to prove herself.

Jinx the cat came trotting toward her from the direction of the barn and threw his heavy body against her legs. Now that he'd had his night out, he was ready for some TLC, so Skye leaned down and scooped him up.

"Well, Jinxy old boy, I struck out again."

The cat butted his head against the underside of her chin as if telling her he had total faith in her. She set the cat on the lodge pole fence, and he trotted easily along the top rail to the next post, where he stopped to groom himself.

Ah, to be carefree.

Although, honestly, Skye didn't need to be carefree. Being a widow had knocked most of the carefree out of her, and she truly doubted that she'd ever get it back. What she wanted was to be secure. Secure enough to not worry about losing her place. Secure enough to provide for her pets and livestock.

Secure enough to not lie awake worrying at night.

Was that too much to ask for?

SOMETHING WAS UP with Tyler's cousin, Blaine Hayward. Whenever he shifted his jaw sideways and did the thousand-mile stare instead of making eye contact—or in this case, watching the high school kids practice bull riding in Hennessey's practice pen—he was dealing with something. And Tyler had a strong suspicion that whatever his cousin was working over in his head involved him. Blaine was dating Angie Salinas from the café, and Skye worked with Angie. Blaine had barely met Tyler's gaze once that day, which meant that Tyler was probably at the center of whatever.

"Something on your mind?" he finally asked after they'd watched the last practice ride.

Blaine shot him a sideways glance, looking relieved at the question. "I heard you offered Skye a loan."

"Where'd you hear that?" Because Tyler couldn't see Skye spreading the word. She had her pride.

"Angie saw the two of you talking yesterday, and asked Skye about it, because...well, you know how things are between you two."

Yeah. He did.

"And Skye told her about the loan?"

Blaine met his gaze then, dead on. "Skye told Angie that you were trying to buy a clear conscience."

It took Tyler a couple of seconds to say, "No kidding." He even managed a fairly reasonable tone, given the circumstances, but he didn't know how much longer he'd be able to do that. Not with his jaw muscles going tighter every second. *Buy a clear conscience? Really, Skye?*

Blaine shrugged his big shoulders. "You know she blames you for Mason's issues."

"Because Mason was such a saint."

"She needs to think so."

Tyler understood that, but still…to accuse him publicly—because anything said to Angie would soon become public—of trying to *buy* a clear conscience when all he'd wanted to do was to help her?

That grated.

Really grated.

"Don't do anything to make me regret telling you this," Blaine muttered. Ty frowned. "I'm serious, man. Angie will kill me."

Ty gave a nod, somehow keeping himself from pointing out that Angie had probably already filled in half the town, which totally ticked him off. He could deal with being the scapegoat for Skye's dead husband's behavior, but he was not going to put up with her spreading blatant rumors about him.

He was going to have a word with Skye. Set the record straight. Most of it, anyway. And he was going to have Skye issue a retraction—via Angie or any other method she chose.

ANY HOPE SKYE had of negotiating a loan with Marshal Valley Bank was squelched the instant she took a seat at the loan officer's desk. Dan Peterson wore "the look"—the one that clearly indicated that he'd investigated matters and, even though his bank was smaller and more lenient in their lending practices than most, and even though they'd known each other since high school, Skye didn't qualify for a second-chance loan. She gave it a shot anyway after they'd exchanged stiff opening pleasantries. She explained the reason for the mortgage, how she and her husband had accidentally overextended, and because of his gambling addiction had lost the fund that was supposed to see them through rough times. She handed over her figures and explained that there would be no more gambling, that her husband was dead and she was trying desperately to hold on to her ranch.

It was obvious that the guy felt for her, and equally obvious that his answer had to be no.

"For now," he'd told her when she'd gotten to her feet. She was used to the rubbery-knee, rock-in-her-stomach feelings by now, so she simply smiled when he said, "Come back in six months, when your payments are current, and we'll talk."

Six months. Dead of winter. When her cows needed the hay. Right.

"I wish I could do more, Skye, but my bosses—"

"I understand, Dan. Thanks."

She drove home, racking her brain as to her next move. She could maybe eke out six months. If nothing happened. If the strange sound in the truck's reverse gear didn't get more persistent. If the animals all stayed healthy. If she could nail down another part-time job, work eighteen-hour days. It wouldn't have to be forever. Just long enough to catch up. But it also wouldn't buy hay for her cattle.

Skye felt tears start to well up, but she blinked them back, suddenly sitting taller in her seat when she saw the truck parked next to her house.

Ty Hayward's truck.

Unless Jess had borrowed it.

Yeah. That had to be it. But when the man got out of the driver's seat as she pulled in, she instantly knew it wasn't Jess. They might be twins, but Ty's movements were different, smoother, more catlike than Jess's. More…predatory.

Ty Hayward had come to call, and she hated to think of what that could mean. She was very certain, however, judging from the grim expression he wore, that he wasn't there to offer her money again.

SKYE STARTED WALKING toward where Ty stood beside his truck, stony expression firmly in place. Her hair was pulled into a sophisticated-looking bun thing instead of tumbling around her shoulders in dark waves as usual, and she wore a light blue dress with sensible heels.

He instantly surmised that she'd been to another bank and that things had not gone well. Ty told himself he didn't care.

"Hello, Tyler." She came to a stop a few feet away from him, just as she had the day before, and adjusted the position of the purse strap on her shoulder, keeping her fingers lightly curled around the black leather.

"Skye."

"What brings you here today?"

Coolly spoken words, but Ty read uncertainty in her expression. Guilt, perhaps…?

"I'm for sure not here to offer you money." He took a lazy step forward. "I want you to set the record straight."

"What record?"

His voice grew hard as he said, "Where do you come off telling people that I'm trying to *buy* a clear conscience?"

Skye gaped at him. "What?"

He cocked his head. "What part needs repeating?"

"I never told anyone you were trying to buy a clear conscience."

"Well, that's the story going around, Skye. I wonder how it started." He didn't need any hints as to how it spread. Angie was something. He took another step forward, doing his best to ignore the fact that she looked utterly confused. "I tried to help you, Skye. I wanted to help you. It had nothing—not *one* thing—to do with my conscience."

Her chin went up at that. "Nothing?"

He shook his head, realizing then just how deeply ingrained her dislike of him was. She was never going to believe anything but the worst of him, and he wasn't going to try to convince her otherwise. "I'm wasting my time here." He turned and started back across the drive toward his truck, cursing his stupidity in driving to her ranch. The damage was done. And realistically, he'd never expected her to be able to make the situation better, but he wanted her to know what she'd done so that she didn't do it again. Mission accomplished.

He jerked the truck door open, and then, because

this could well be the last time they ever spoke, he said, "For the record, I never gambled with your husband."

An expression of patent disbelief crossed Skye's face, but before she could speak, he said, "I know it's really handy to blame me, since you've never cared for me. I'm a nice, easy target to make you feel better about things, but here's the deal—I don't gamble."

"Ever?"

"More like never as in…never."

"You're saying my husband lied to me."

Sorry, Mason, but the roosters have come home to roost. "I'm saying he used me as an excuse."

"You never partied with him."

"Of course I partied with him. We drank together. A lot. But we never went gambling."

She looked at him as if he was missing the point. "If Mason had stayed in at night, if he hadn't drunk too much, then he wouldn't have gambled. But would you leave him alone? No."

"He never once said anything about wanting to stay in." That was the honest truth. "He never acted like he wanted to stay in." And Tyler hadn't seen the danger of encouraging him to go out until it was too late. But Mason would have gone out no matter what. Tyler was convinced of that.

"Or you're not presenting things the way they really were."

Ty's eyes narrowed. "Why would I present things any other way?" In other words, why would he lie?

"I don't know. Guilt, maybe? Public image?"

"I'm not lying, Skye. I know you believe that I'm the reason you're broke. I'm the reason Mason had hangovers. Yes, you asked me to leave him alone. No,

I didn't do it. But I didn't encourage him to gamble and lose all of his money—or to gamble some more to try to make it all back. That was fully his thing."

Tyler's jaw tightened as he fought the urge to tell Skye the whole truth. To tell her what her husband was like on the road. To tell her that gambling wasn't the only vice Mason indulged in.

But angry as he was, he couldn't do that to her.

He also couldn't handle being in her presence any longer. "You want to hide behind a lie? Fine. Have a good life, Skye." The words came out bitterly, as if he cared in some way about what she thought, but he didn't.

"You, too," Skye said in a stony voice, before walking past him, her heels tilting in the gravel as she made her way around his truck. She was almost directly in front of the vehicle when she stopped dead in her tracks.

Ty followed her line of vision and instantly saw the problem. One of her horses was down, next to the water trough, and from the way it was lying with its neck stretched out and its head at an odd angle, he didn't think it was napping. He got back out of his truck at the same moment that Skye started running toward the pasture in her heels.

He might be angry. He might have been happy to never see Skye again. But no way was he going to drive away when she had a horse down.

The horse needed help even if Skye didn't.

Chapter Four

Mr. Joe lay stretched out on the ground next to the water tank, and even as Skye raced toward him, she knew it was too late. She slid to a stop close to his head, dropping to her knees in the dirt and reaching out to stroke his face. His eye came open and rolled up at her. He blinked once and shut his eyes again as he gave a rattling breath.

"No, no, no." Skye barely registered what she was saying as she stroked his ears and then wrapped her arms around his neck, burying her face against him, pulling in his scent. This day had been coming. Mr. Joe hadn't been able to hold weight for the past year, despite her best efforts and bags and bags of senior horse chow, but, dignified gentleman that he was, he'd never shown any sign of weakness or pain. He'd eaten what he could and spent his days ambling around the pasture, hanging with his best buddy, Pepper, or just sleeping in the sun.

Tyler dropped down beside her, checking the horse's pulse at his throat and then running a gentle hand over the animal's jowl as his gaze traveled over the horse's bony frame.

"How old?"

"Twenty-eight." The words stuck in Skye's throat. She swallowed and said, "I knew it was coming, but I'm not ready yet." As if she'd ever be ready.

She jerked her gaze away from Tyler's before tears could form. Why did he have to be here for this? But he was here and her horse was dying and she had to deal. Again she rested her cheek against her old gentleman's neck and squeezed her eyes shut, blocking out. Denying. She felt the last breath. Felt him go still, but she did not move. Could not move. Mr. Joe had been with her since she was ten. He'd been her 4-H horse, her very slow rodeo horse, her friend, confidant. Companion. After Mason had died, she'd spent hours grooming the old gelding, talking to him, mourning his weight loss and the inevitable, but loving him while he was there to love.

Now the inevitable had happened, and another big hole opened up in her heart.

Tears now soaked the old horse's mane, and her cheek felt grimy from the pasture dust sticking to it. She blinked hard again, then pushed back onto her knees, small rocks biting into her flesh as she ran her hand over the gelding's soft coat one more time.

She knew Tyler stood a few feet away now, but she kept her eyes on the horse. He'd best not try to touch her, comfort her. She didn't need other people to help her deal with her loss. She was a master.

And there was always the fear that she would break down if she had the luxury of human contact as she mourned. When she'd lost Mason, people had gathered near, helping in any way they could, while she was still numb, still going through the motions. It wasn't until she was once again alone that the pain had ripped through her, burning in its intensity as she faced an empty ranch, empty house, empty bed.

Tyler moved a few steps toward her, then stopped as she shot him a look.

He let out a breath, pressed his lips together. There were lines of strain on his face, as if he wasn't certain what to say or do. There was nothing he could say or do. Her horse was gone, and he was there when she didn't want him to be.

"Do you want me to call Jess?"

"Why?"

"He's better with the backhoe than I am."

The backhoe. He was going to help her bury Mr. Joe. "I…uh…" She wiped the back of her hand across her damp, sticky cheeks, then lifted her chin as new tears threatened. "I'll call Cliff." Her five-mile-down-the-road neighbor.

Tyler's expression hardened. "Or Jess and I could bury your gelding."

"I'm not trying to be ungrateful." But it was her right at the moment as grief once again wrapped around her.

"You just want me off the property. I get it. Wish granted." He turned and headed toward his truck.

TYLER SMACKED THE steering wheel with the heel of his hand as he waited at the crossroad for a slow-moving cattle truck. Always the bad guy. He was getting pretty sick of being the bad guy—especially when he hadn't done anything. Okay, he'd purposely defied Skye, but not in a way meant to do her harm. Everybody partied while on the road, and Mason would have been as likely to stay in his hotel room when everyone else was having a grand old time as he would have been likely to quit bull riding to become an accountant.

Tyler pulled out onto the gravel road, debating about whether to call Jess and tell him to go bury the old horse, or whether to let Skye handle it on her own. He'd hated leaving her alone, but it seemed as if staying would have made her even more unhappy.

He'd tried to be nice. Twice. He was done.

Jess wasn't there when he got home after a quick stop at the grocery store.

He let himself into the unlocked trailer, set down the bags and opened the tiny cupboard next to the stove. There was a reason he was eating out more than he should. It was hard to cook in the camp trailer, and even harder to keep enough food on hand. He had to step over his gear as he made his way to the kitchen, so he stopped and pushed it out of his way with his foot as best he could. He wasn't crazy neat, like his brother, but even he was getting tired of stepping over and around everything in order to move through their living space.

He had to get out of there while he and his brother were still on speaking terms—that was a given. His first event was in two weeks, but sometimes he had his doubts as to whether they would last that long. Jess was a peaceful guy, but even he had his limits, and living in close contact with his twin was pushing them. Tyler opened the cupboard, then closed it again and leaned his forehead against the fake wood.

When a guy was a winner, he shouldn't feel so much like a loser. What was he doing here in this tiny trailer, making his brother feel cramped and uncomfortable?

Ty shoved the full bag of perishables into the fridge

and then left the trailer. He needed to move, try to shake this thing that kept bothering him…whatever that thing was.

It took him only a few miles of road to pinpoint the thing.

Being wrongly accused. He hadn't tried to keep Mason on the straight and narrow, but he hadn't encouraged him to stray either. Not in gambling, nor in any other way. He'd just been a friend. Someone to party with. If it hadn't been him, then it would have been someone else. Mason rode hard and played hard. As far as he knew, he was a good husband to Skye— except for when he wasn't.

The parking lot at the Shamrock was full. Tyler parked close to his usual spot in the wide gravel parking lot behind the building but didn't get out of the truck immediately. Did he want to socialize?

The fact that he was questioning the matter told him no. He did not. Rare, but it happened, especially when something was eating at him.

He leaned his head back against the seat rest, half closed his eyes and watched as people came in and out of the back door of the establishment. When he saw Shelly Hensley go in, he made his decision. No socializing tonight. Shelly was banned from the place, and he wasn't up for the ruckus that would ensue when the owner, Thad Hawkins, or his nephew, Gus, escorted her from the premises.

Decision made, he reached for the ignition.

Was he getting old?

No way. He was just not in as much of a mood to socialize as he'd thought he was. He'd go back to the trailer, eat something, crawl into his bunk and read. In the morning he'd go for his run, then hit up some Realtors and do his best to find a place to buy before he let his winnings trickle through his fingers…and before he and his brother came to blows. The last time he'd won big money, he'd made a healthy donation to the recovery of a fellow bull rider, a guy with a new baby and a toddler, and a broken back. He didn't expect to see that money back anytime soon—which was why he needed to invest his new winnings now. While he had the money in hand and before another of his friends got seriously injured. He wasn't a light touch, but a friend in need got whatever Ty could give.

He'd barely touched the key when someone knocked loudly on the back of his truck and then a familiar face pushed against the window, features distorted through the glass. Tyler lowered the window, forcing Cody Callahan to jerk back. The kid was eight years younger than him, and an up-and-comer on the bull-riding circuit.

"How many times do I got to tell you not to beat on my truck?" he asked.

"I needed to get your attention." Cody jerked his head in the direction of the back door of the Shamrock. "Going in or coming out?"

Tyler debated for a second. "Going in." Now that he had company, he may as well make a night of it.

"Then shake a leg, man." Cody stepped back so that Tyler could open the door. "I'm parched."

HUMBLE PIE NEVER tasted good. Today it was going to taste like ashes, but Skye was going to eat it and smile. As well as she could, anyway. She was working the second half of the morning shift that day, having traded shifts with her pregnant coworker, Chloe, but she'd called Angie at the café just before opening and asked the question that had weighed on her mind for a good part of the night. Well, yes, Angie confessed, maybe she had told Blaine that Tyler was trying to buy himself a clear conscience by offering the loan. And…yeah… it was possible she'd mentioned it to other people. No, she wouldn't say anything else about the matter…but it was probably too late.

No kidding.

Skye had hung up knowing that Tyler was right about one thing—she should have sidestepped Angie's question about why she and Tyler were talking near her car instead of telling her the truth and providing rumor fodder—but in all honesty, she'd hoped that Angie might know of someone who could help her obtain financing. After all, Angie knew everyone. How on earth was Skye to know that the woman would put her own spin on the matter? Usually she gossiped verbatim.

Things will blow over. Somebody will do something gossip-worthy. It'd been a while since Shelly Hensley had picked a fight in public. Maybe she'd do something spectacular and then everyone would forget about Skye and Tyler. Regardless, she felt as if she owed Ty an apology for the rumor. She may not have spread it, but there was no getting around the fact that—whether he did it out of guilt or generosity—he'd tried to help and she'd conveyed the wrong message to Angie, expressing amazement at his nerve when she'd discussed the situation, and Angie had eaten it up.

After finishing her morning chores, Skye let herself into the house and walked through her sparkling-clean kitchen to pour a cup of coffee. The coffeemaker gleamed and there wasn't one water spot on the carafe, but cleaning everything she could get her hands on last night hadn't done much to take the edge off the pain caused by losing her equine friend, or to still the whispers of doubt that had been growing louder as the hours passed.

Mason hadn't lied to her about Tyler…had he?

His only lies—and they had been major—had been by omission. He'd neglected to tell her about his growing gambling problem—he probably would have never told her if he hadn't won a huge check and brought home exactly nothing. All of his winnings had been lost on a casino table in one unlucky roll of the dice. He'd tried to defend himself; tried to explain that since he'd dislocated his shoulder during the ride, he probably wouldn't have gotten another big check that season. He'd needed to double their money.

Skye had simply stared at him as they sat together in their hotel room, wondering who this man was. How he could have made such a reckless move with their future. When asked that question, he'd broken down, explained that he had a growing problem. It wasn't the first time he'd gambled, but usually he either won or broke even. His record had given him confidence. What were the chances of losing everything when he'd played so carefully and consistently?

That was when they'd mortgaged the ranch, because the ranch fund had been too small to save them, and Mason had sworn he wouldn't gamble—that he wouldn't even go out in the evenings. He'd stay in his hotel room or in the camper. Watch TV, play video games.

When he had gone out, instead of staying in his room, he'd confessed, as if Skye had spies. She hadn't. He was her husband and she trusted him, so when he said that he went out only because of Tyler's relentless needling, she believed him. Since he brought home his checks when he won—the actual checks—and handed them over to Skye, she had no reason to believe he was gambling. No reason to suspect that he'd tapped into the ranch fund.

It had been a little after midnight and deep into the cleaning when she acknowledged to herself that, if Mason had secretly emptied the ranch fund because of his addiction, he might also have lied about Tyler. He might have needed an excuse in case he was seen at the tables. He was there watching Tyler gamble.

She may be totally off base. Tyler could be guilty, but they had to live together in this small community, and on the off chance that he was innocent, she was going to apologize for that, too. Make nice. End this thing between them once and for all.

Skye sipped her coffee, then pushed it aside. It tasted like acid.

Decision made, she picked up her purse and headed for the door, pausing on the porch to stare off across the field to where faithful Mr. Joe lay. Cliff had operated the backhoe for her—her skills there had never been beyond beginner basics—and helped her bury her horse in his favorite sunning place in the pasture.

Her throat started to close up again, but Skye swallowed the big lump and headed for her car. She didn't think she had any tears left to shed, but one never knew and she didn't need her eyes any more swollen than they already were—especially if she was going to confront Tyler Hayward.

Chapter Five

Tyler's head came up off the pillow as the beating sound intensified, but he was having trouble opening his eyes. When he finally pried one lid open, he realized that someone was knocking on the trailer door. Short intense raps that seemed to echo in his head.

"Get that, would you?" Jess called from the back of the trailer. He sounded the way Ty felt. Like crap.

"Yeah." The word croaked out of his throat. "Coming," he yelled as he shoved his legs into his jeans.

He heard the sound of retreating footsteps as he approached the door, stumbling over his boots on the way. Whoever had been at the door was leaving, but since he was now vertical and semidressed, he figured he may as well see who the visitor was. Pushing open the door, he stepped out onto the small landing his brother had built out of scrap lumber. Skye Larkin was walking toward her car, which was parked where his pickup would be if he hadn't left it at the Shamrock and caught a ride home with Blaine.

"Hey."

Skye stopped dead, her back going stiff, before she slowly turned. And even though he was sore at her, he couldn't help but think, as always, how ridiculously beautiful she was.

"Hi," she said, her voice almost as stiff as her back. She started back toward him, keeping her eyes firmly on his face. Apparently she didn't want to admire the wonder of his naked torso. Well, women who didn't want to see half-naked men shouldn't knock on their doors at unearthly hours.

"Can I help you with something?" His words were clipped, his voice cold. Couldn't help himself.

"You can accept my apology."

Unexpected, to say the least. Especially since she'd apparently made a special trip to do so. "You're apologizing?"

She came to a stop close to the bottom step, and since Tyler didn't feel right looking down at her, he started down the steps. Skye took a measured step back, and he stopped. "I am. I was rude yesterday."

"Your horse died."

Her eyes were red and puffy, as he imagined his were. He didn't drink that often anymore, because it interfered with his training, but last night he'd made up for lost time.

"Yes. Well, regardless, sorry. I shouldn't have told Angie about the loan…but you need to know that I'm not responsible for the buy-the-clear-conscience bit."

He narrowed his eyes at her. If she wasn't responsible for the part that had offended him, then he had only one question. "Why the apology, Skye?"

"Did some thinking last night."

"And realized you needed the loan."

The expression that crossed her face, the way she blinked as if she'd just been slapped, made *him* feel like apologizing, except that he'd done nothing wrong. He'd offered her a loan. He'd offered to help bury her horse. He was not the bad guy.

"This has nothing to do with the loan," she snapped. "Except for the part that Angie embellished." She glared at him briefly, then turned and stalked toward her car. Tyler fought with himself until she was almost there, then bounded down off the porch, making his head throb a little. She heard him coming and stopped with her hand on the car's door handle. She turned on him with another killer glare and said, "What?"

He regarded her for a moment. Her nose wrinkled a little, and he realized he probably smelled like a brewery. Tough. "I want to know something, Skye. What do you have against me?" She opened her mouth, then closed it again. Her jaw muscles went tight as if she was working very hard to keep words from spilling out.

"Too many things to articulate?" he asked with mock innocence. His voice hardened as he asked, "Do you need the money I offered you, Skye?"

"That's not why I came."

"And that's not an answer."

She closed her eyes as she let out a breath, her dark lashes fanning over her cheeks as she debated responses.

"The truth will do just fine, Skye."

Her eyes flashed open. Blue fire. "Yes. I need the money."

"What happens if you don't get it?"

"I'll probably lose the truck and...I don't know about the ranch. Depends if I can get another job."

"Two jobs?"

She nodded, her lips now clamped firmly shut. Tyler

raised his eyes to the horizon. The sun was well above the tree line. Maybe it wasn't such an unearthly hour after all. He breathed deeply, drawing in the scent of grass and pines and Skye. Something in him stirred, and he told it to stop.

When he looked back at Skye, she was eyeing him warily, as if she were teetering on the brink of something and he had the power to tip her one way or the other. She hated it. He could tell.

He forced the corners of his mouth up. They fought him, but he got the job done. "I won't give you the loan…but I'll buy into your operation."

Skye's chin jerked up. "Wh-what?"

"I owe it to Mason. He was my friend—whom I did not gamble with." He needed to make that last part clear. "Here's the deal. I'll become your partner. I will infuse cash into your cattle operation, help you catch up on your payments."

"What do you get out of it?" Skye asked.

"Half your profits."

"Then you won't get much."

"And I want a place to live."

Her eyes flashed, and then she held up her palms as if to ward him off. "You are not moving into my house."

"I'll move a trailer onto the place."

"With Jess?" There was a hopeful note in her voice that irritated him.

"No, Skye. The whole point of this is to not live with my brother." He rubbed the side of his face.

"I need more details. Like…how long will we be partners?"

"Until you buy me out again."

"For the original amount?"

"That wouldn't be very good business."

"Two percent interest?"

"Three." Which still wasn't that great of a return, but, in truth, he wasn't a very good businessman.

"I need time to think. And I need more concrete terms."

"Three days," Tyler said. "If you're still interested, we meet with C.J. and iron out the terms. I'll make the appointment today."

"And cancel if I say no?"

She wasn't going to do that. He was almost certain that she couldn't—not unless some white knight appeared on the horizon. "Sure. I'll cancel if you say no."

She gave her head a small shake, as if unable to believe she was in this situation. She was—and it was not a situation of his making, regardless of what she might think.

"Hey, Skye…"

She looked up at him, only this time her gaze skimmed over his bare chest, pausing at the scar on his left pectoral muscle, before moving up to his face.

"I'll be gone a lot of the time. Most of the time. Consider that while you make your decision."

"Yes." She lifted her chin, a faint frown pulling her delicate dark eyebrows together. "I will consider that."

SKYE'S HANDS WERE shaking on the steering wheel as she pulled out of the parking place. Anger? Gratitude? Lust?

Because while Mason had been a hard-body, Tyler was incredible. And she was using his incredible physique to distract herself from the issue at hand. He had just offered to buy into her operation. Tyler Hayward. Bad influence. Bane of her existence.

Savior?

It was too much to take in, so she blanked out her mind as best she could and drove to work, parking in the same spot where Tyler had accosted her a day ago—incredible how quickly time flew by—and offered her a loan.

She gave a small snort as she locked her car. She should have swallowed her pride and taken it. It would have put her in a better position than she was in now. How could she let him live on her property? What kind of life would that be, going about her business, caring for her animals, with Tyler there?

One that she may have to endure because unless some miracle came out of nowhere in the next three days, that was exactly what was going to happen.

Maybe Tyler's offer is the miracle.

Was this what her life had come to? A place where Tyler Hayward was her miracle?

She jerked open the back door of the café and stepped into the small room that led to the kitchen. She hung up her sweater, pulled her freshly laundered apron out of her tote bag and tied it on.

He might be her miracle, and she might be grateful to the soles of her shoes, but it was never going to sit well with her. He said he was doing this for Mason. Probably out of guilt.

Yes.

She yanked the bow at the back of her apron tight.

That was it. Guilt.

She could live with that motivation. It wouldn't make it any easier having him on the place, but she could save her money, maybe get that second job she'd talked about. Pay him back super fast.

Get her ranch back…get her life back, such as it was.

"Are you okay?" Chloe called from the register, frowning at Skye's puffy face. A night of cleaning and crying did no one any good.

"My horse died yesterday."

"Ooh." Chloe wrung her hands together then settled them on top of her pregnant belly. "I'm so sorry."

Skye nodded in acknowledgment rather than speak and risk tearing up. Chloe reached down and pulled Skye's notepad out from under the counter.

"Kind of empty today," Skye said as she slipped the book into her apron pocket. As in totally empty, which was a bummer. Tips wouldn't go far in helping her out of her present situation—but they would put some gas in her car.

"The breakfast rush was good. Thanks for letting me work that half of your shift. I'll split the tips with you."

"Not necessary. I'm sure lunch will be good, too." Skye traded Chloe shifts, or half shifts, if necessary, on the days Chloe had OB appointments, and today it had worked out because after her cleaning frenzy, Skye had fallen into bed around 3:00 a.m. and managed a couple hours' sleep, which she wouldn't have gotten had she opened at 5:00 a.m.—even though she'd been awake at that time and on the phone with Angie.

Speaking of which…

"Where's Angie?"

"She's running a quick errand. Something to do with her sister's wedding. She should be back any minute now."

Skye hoped it wouldn't be awkward, just the two of them and no customers, but knowing Angie, she'd already moved on from their early morning conversation.

"Angie said that Tyler offered you a loan." Skye waited, but instead of mentioning the clear-conscience aspect, Chloe shot her a curious look as she undid her apron and slipped it over her head. "Is everything okay?"

"Couldn't be better," Skye said. Then, figuring she may as well start her own rumors and have them be truthful, she added, "We're going into business together."

The heavy ceramic mug Chloe was holding slipped out of her hands, landing with a thud on the Formica countertop. "What kind of business?"

"Ranching." Skye looked past Chloe to an older couple that had just pushed through the door. "I'd better seat them."

Skye seated the couple, got them water and menus, then drifted back to the register. "Nothing firm yet, but we're in discussions."

"Why would you do that?" Chloe asked, sounding genuinely concerned.

Skye smiled at her. It felt like a weary smile, a smile one might find on a woman who'd lived for eighty decades instead of almost three. "Sometimes life backs you into a corner and all you can do is graciously say yes when someone offers you a way out."

"I DON'T SEE this ending well," Jess said to Tyler as they stood side by side, leaning against the rails of Hennessey's outdoor practice pen. Bull-riding practice would move to the indoor facility once the weather grew inclement, but Ty didn't think he'd be home all that often during that time, but if he was home it was going to be grand having a place to live where he wasn't practically on top of his brother. That was the only part of the plan that Jess did fully approve of.

"I'm not taking advantage of her. I'm helping her in the only way she can accept."

"Offer her the loan again."

"No."

"Why?" Jess tipped back his hat as he turned to eye his brother.

"Because this works for both of us. Skye gets out from under the debt and I get a place to put my money."

"And a place to live."

"The best part of all." He raised his chin as the chute across the pen opened and a young riderless bull charged out, twisting and bucking. "He has potential."

"That he does. I like the new lines Hennessey is breeding."

So did Tyler, although he'd be retired from riding before most of the young stock was ready to buck for real. Once the young bull had disappeared through the gate and the crew started loading another, Tyler shot his brother a look. "You know that I'm grateful that you gave me a roof. I'd do the same for you."

"If things don't start looking up, that may happen sooner than you think."

Jess's job wasn't all that stable, which was one reason he was living as cheaply as possible, and in Ty's way of thinking, that opened up opportunity. "Then you can try your luck on the circuit guilt free. You aren't shirking your duty. Your duty shirked you."

Jess was not impressed with his brother's argument.

"Look." He paused, and Tyler prepared himself for the lecture. "Look" followed by a silence meant something important was about to be imparted.

"Don't do anything to mess up Skye's life. She's had enough trouble."

Tyler waited for the rest. Nothing. He tilted his head, frowning a little. "Do you honestly think I want to mess up Skye's life?"

"I know you're irritated at her for thinking the worst of you."

"Totally guilty." He looked back across the arena as a bull came down the alleyway. "But I see this as an investment and a business proposition. If Skye's life gets screwed up, so does mine."

Chapter Six

Skye felt numb as she left the lawyer's office a little less than two weeks after Tyler had made his proposal to her. *This is the lesser of two evils.* It was either go into partnership with Tyler, hope for a miracle—which hadn't worked out all that well so far—or lose the ranch a little at a time.

"Cheer up," Tyler said, lightly tapping her on the arm with the rolled-up papers he carried as they walked together down the tiled hallway toward the exit. "I'm back on the circuit in a week. You'll barely see me."

"Except when you're here."

"That's no way to talk to your partner," he said mildly, but she sensed steel just under the surface of the comment.

Okay, so her tone wasn't the most gracious, but she was still coming to terms with the situation. "Sorry," she muttered.

Tyler put a hand on her shoulder, and she instantly stopped walking, but he didn't drop his hand immediately. The casual contact made her feel way too aware of him, which Skye didn't like one bit. She couldn't help it—Tyler made her jumpy.

"I don't want your sorry."

Too late. She swallowed the retort. "You're right. We need to work together. I appreciate your stepping in to help me out." She sounded sincere, and she was... except she couldn't help dwelling on the fact that her copies of the legal agreement were carefully filed in her dad's tooled leather briefcase, which she'd dug out for the occasion. Tyler's were rolled in a tube, which he carried loosely in one hand and would probably soon toss into the backseat of his pickup. They were so different—and, in many ways, he was so much like Mason—how on earth were they going to partner successfully?

Compromise.

Except that she didn't want to compromise on her own ranch.

It isn't your ranch anymore...not until you buy him out.

The truth hurt.

"How do you suggest we proceed?" she asked as he dropped his hand, making Skye feel as if she'd suddenly been set free.

"As carefully as possible." When she frowned at him, he said, "I worked up a plan. Maybe when I get done moving my trailer onto the property, we can go over said plan."

"Sure." Skye couldn't say that she liked the idea of Tyler making plans. In fact, knowing that he was formulating plans for her—their—ranch made her feel even more territorial. Sucking in a breath, she started for the door, which Tyler opened for her. "When do you think that will be?"

"Tomorrow. When you get off shift."

"Tomorrow is my day off."

"Great. You can help me skirt my trailer."

"Happy to." *Was this really happening?* She couldn't help a quick glance at him and saw that he wasn't fooled by her show of positivity.

They walked down the sidewalk to the parking lot. Tyler's truck was on the far west and hers was on the far east. She hadn't planned it that way, but it worked for her. Tyler stopped at the point where their paths diverged, hooking his thumbs in his belt loops. He hesitated for a moment, then said, "I know you hate this, but as I see it, it was me or the highway."

He understood her situation exactly—but it would have been hard not to. It wasn't as if she were dodging the facts or misrepresenting anything. Tyler and his newly hired accountant had gone over her tax and ranch records for the past several years. He knew her situation, and he knew what he was getting into.

"You're correct." This was the eating-humble-pie part that she hated so much.

"I want this ranch to work. If that means sorting out what needs to be done and assigning responsibilities, so that we don't get in each other's way, that's what we'll do." He stepped a little closer, and Skye's breath caught. She wasn't used to being this close to Tyler Hayward. For years she'd done her best to stay far away from him.

"Actually, the ranch runs pretty well."

"Meaning…?"

"I can run the ranch just fine on my own. I've done it for years. You can take your half of the profits. You'll have a place to stay."

He smiled. "You're essentially demoting me from partner to tenant?"

His tone told her it wasn't going to happen. He wouldn't let her run her ranch alone. She quirked one corner of her mouth up into a grim half smile. "If I thought you'd let me, I'd do it in a heartbeat."

"What makes you think I won't let you?"

"You want me to squirm."

His expression shifted ever so slightly. She'd struck a nerve.

"Your ideas of my motivations are off base."

"Maybe so," she allowed, even though she didn't believe it. Fighting with her "partner" wasn't conducive to peaceful coexistence until she could buy him out. "Habit. I'll work on it."

"I'm moving the trailer in tonight. I'll see you tomorrow to discuss our partnership. What time works for you?"

"Eight o'clock." She wanted to get it over with. Yes, it was going to mess with her day, but she needed to get used to Tyler messing with her days. "I'll see you then."

Determined to have the last word, she turned on her heel and almost twisted her ankle. Somehow she managed the first few steps in the direction of her car without limping, because she knew for a fact that Tyler was watching. Watching her and quite possibly smiling that…*smile* of his. The crooked one that made her feel off-kilter and self-conscious.

Yes. That smile.

Well, maybe working with her on the ranch would help wipe that smile off his face.

AT LEAST SHE hadn't fallen when her heel caught, because if she had, then Tyler would have had to fight instinct and let her pick herself back up. Skye Larkin wanted as little to do with him as possible, and because she was now beholden, she was all the more determined to keep him at arm's length.

He dug his keys out of his pocket and headed for his truck. *Too bad, babe.* He was her partner, and they were going to tune up the ranch so that it made money. Things wouldn't change that radically, but he had some ideas and there was a boatload of repairs to make around the place. He wouldn't have a lot of time to do those himself, but he could hire them done if he continued winning.

He saw no reason why he wouldn't. Winning was what he did.

The trailer he'd bought used was almost twice the size of the one his brother was living in. He'd offered to trade, because he was going to be home a heck of a lot less often than Jess, but Jess had said no. He'd earn his own bigger trailer. Tyler didn't fight him. He liked the new-to-him trailer and figured he'd be comfortable there when he wasn't on the road and his twin would have adequate space in his own home now that he wasn't sharing.

Less than two hours after signing the legal agreement, Tyler and Blaine parked the trailer on the far side of the dilapidated bunkhouse, where he had access to sewage, power and water lines. All the niceties of home—most of which he'd lacked in his early days on the road when he'd dry camped. Now he drove or flew to his events and stayed in motels and hotels more often than not. It was good to be in the money, to be comfortable on the road.

The trick was to stay in the money. The one given in a bull rider's career was that it could end at any time—

or, at the very least, be subject to an extended hiatus. He'd been blessed with a relatively injury-free season so far, which he attributed to luck and his more intense training and eating regime. Nothing like winning big to motivate a guy to do it again.

"I can't believe you're going to live here," Blaine said as he dusted his hands off, then lifted his chin as the little donkey they'd put back into the pasture twice came trotting toward them again. "That little guy needs to be in sheep wire."

The mule, who was apparently the little guy's bosom buddy, leaned over the fence and called for his friend.

"My turn," Tyler said as he headed toward the donkey.

"Should we leave him out? We can keep an eye on him."

"And listen to that?" Tyler called back, his voice nearly drowned out by plaintive mule cries.

"Good point."

Tyler easily caught the donkey and after a moment's thought led him toward the barn, where he put him into a small pen that opened out onto the pasture. The mule trotted toward the pen, and the two were soon bonding over the planks. Tyler wondered how long it would be before the little Houdini figured a way out of the pen. Apparently he stayed in the pasture on the honor system when Skye wasn't home—not a big surprise given how loose the wire was on most of the fences.

"We should have done that in the first place," Tyler said as he rejoined Blake by the trailer. They stood for a moment regarding the ranch, and Tyler was fairly certain that Blake saw exactly what he did—a ranch that had been something back in the day, and could once again be something, but not without an infusion of cash. Tyler's cash.

"Are you sure about this?" Blake finally asked.

"I had to invest in something. This seemed good."

"Because of what Mason did?"

This again. Tyler stopped adjusting a hose and gave his cousin a hard look. "Because Skye shouldn't lose her ranch due to his...indiscretions."

Blaine pushed his hat back. "You going all white knight?"

Tyler smirked up at him from where he knelt in the dirt. "I think the princess welcomes the arrival of the white knight." He went back to work on the clamp. "I'm investing my money."

Blaine looked around. "I've seen better investments."

"The place is a little run-down. A lot of places are." The droughts of recent years had been ruthless, but the weather seemed to have shifted last year, and for the first time in ages they had a normal snowpack, which meant normal water, which meant better production.

The ranch wasn't a bad investment. He wouldn't let it be. When he wasn't on the road, he'd help Skye work the place, and when he was, she was more than capable of handling things. Probably more capable than he was in some ways. She knew the place. She'd grown up there. It was going to take her a while to get used to having him around, but as he saw it, she'd better get used to it, because it was also going to take her a while to buy him out. Ty was very curious to see how things played out between them.

So was Blaine. "I hope you guys don't kill each other or something."

"We'll do fine…after the initial period of adjustment."

And that, he had a feeling, was going to be interesting.

SKYE DECIDED THE best place to meet with Tyler to go over his plan for the future of her ranch…which was actually now *their* ranch, as much as that pained her… was at the old picnic table in her yard. That way she wouldn't get that trapped-with-Tyler feeling. Being in a small space with the guy, like her kitchen, made her feel edgy and self-conscious, and that was the last thing she wanted. This first meeting would set the tone for their working relationship, and she wanted every advantage.

At eight o'clock she came out of the house with a carafe of coffee, two cups and a small pan of warm take-and-bake cinnamon rolls. As she unloaded the items from the tray she'd used to carry them, Tyler came up the walk.

"Wouldn't it have been easier to meet in your kitchen?"

"But it's so nice out here," she said lightly as she poured a cup of coffee. She raised her eyebrows at him politely as she gestured to the second cup.

"Please." He sat down on the bench on the opposite side of the table from where she stood. She poured the coffee and pushed the tin of rolls closer to him. He shook his head, and she gave him a curious look.

"I watch what I eat. No useless carbs."

Skye blinked at him. How was she supposed to enjoy eating her roll when someone with a nutritional conscience was sitting across the table from her?

"That gets you no points in my book," she murmured as she maneuvered her way onto the bench.

"Nutrition plays a big part in building muscle mass," he said as he took a drink of coffee. "Why don't you want me in your kitchen?"

She ignored the question, because there was no way she was giving a truthful answer to it, and defiantly pulled a cinnamon roll out of the pan and set it on the napkin in front of her. Tyler's stomach rumbled audibly, and she almost smiled.

"What did you have for breakfast?" she asked as she took a bite of the flaky roll.

"Four eggs. But that was almost three hours ago."

He had eaten at five?

He read the question in her face and gave a casual shrug. "I wanted to take a look at the place."

"Without me." As soon as she spoke, Skye wished she could take the words back. He had a half interest in the place. He could do whatever he wanted.

"I didn't know if you were awake."

"I work the early shift at the café, so I'm usually up at five."

"Good to know."

Skye didn't know why. It wasn't like they'd be doing anything together. As she understood it, the point of this meeting was to delineate responsibilities so that they could stay out of each other's way. "You said you have a plan."

"Nothing on paper, but I do have an idea or two."

Skye took another bite of the roll, but she barely tasted it, which was a shame, because she rarely indulged. Tyler set down his cup. "You've run this ranch for a long time essentially on your own."

"True."

"It's not in very good shape." She opened her mouth to defend herself, but Tyler raised his eyebrows and she closed it again, figuring it was better to let him finish insulting her and then mount a defense. "Which is no surprise given the circumstances."

She bit into the cinnamon roll, then slowly chewed, glad to have a reason not to speak.

"The outbuildings need to be reroofed. There are fencing issues. The corrals haven't been cleaned in a long time."

Skye swallowed and dabbed at her lips with the paper napkin. "Anything else?"

"I didn't have a lot of time to look at the equipment—"

"It's all fairly new. We invested after Mason won those big back-to-back checks three years ago."

"Good use of the money."

"Better than some of his other uses," she said, her mild tone belying the tightening in her chest. Mason's betrayal was still difficult for her to both fathom and forgive.

"I'm sorry this happened to you, Skye." Tyler spoke softly. Sincerely. As if he understood and sympathized. Skye didn't want sympathy any more than she wanted him on the ranch.

She set what was left of the cinnamon roll aside. "It's done and I haven't lost the ranch." She propped her elbows on the table in front of her. "What else?"

"I got winter hay for a good price from Blaine. He'll deliver while I'm gone."

"That's good." Even though she hated feeling as if the ranch operations were being taken out of her hands.

"And, since you're working and I'll be gone a good deal of the time, I decided that we should hire out the fence and roof repairs."

"*You* decided." She couldn't help herself. She hated having all of the decisions taken out of her hands.

"Here's the deal, Skye. I have the money to do the repairs *now*. If I get hurt, then I won't have an income. My idea is to pour as much into the ranch as possible now, so that it can start making money and then I'll have something to fall back onto."

Talk about déjà vu. Mason had said the exact same thing when they'd first married and started planning their future. He'd meant what he said, until gambling took over his life and common sense. She was sure that Tyler meant what he said—for now. But how long would this aura of responsibility last before circumstances, and good times on the road, caused it to dissipate?

She swallowed her rising annoyance and said in a stony voice, "That makes sense."

It also made sense for her to get that second job and do everything she could to buy her ranch back as soon as possible.

"Since I'm paying for half of the repairs, maybe I should have half a say in matters."

"I planned to pay for the repairs."

"That isn't the way our agreement is written." It was very clearly a fifty-fifty deal for cash outlay.

"I want the repairs made soon."

"And I want to wait until I can pay fifty percent of those repairs."

"Realistically, Skye, how long will it be before you can do that?"

She shifted on the bench. "I think we both know it won't be this fall."

"Let me do this. It only makes sense, and because I'll be gone, all of the day-to-day stuff falls to you. It seems fair."

Skye's mouth flattened. "I don't—"

"Like to be beholden?"

"There's that."

"And the fact that you don't much like your business partner."

"How am I supposed to answer that, Tyler?"

"Let's try the truth."

She chewed the inside of her cheek. Debated. "All right…how comfortable do you think I am being partners with a guy I accused of…" She made a gesture instead of finishing the sentence. He knew what she'd accused him of. "A guy I never got along with all that well in the first place."

"Why is that, Skye?"

She couldn't help the incredulous stare. "You're really asking that?"

"Yeah. I am. Because I never understood."

Now who was kidding whom? "Where do I begin?"

He put his elbow on the table and propped his chin in his hand. "Anyplace will do." His tone was one of casual interest, but there was a hard glint in his eyes.

Skye closed her own eyes briefly. Where *could* she begin and how could it possibly help things now? It couldn't help, so she wasn't opening this particular can of worms. Wasn't going to risk showing any vulnerabilities to this man—like the fact that she'd been intimidated by him back in the day.

She opened her eyes and found him studying her

face, his expression intent, as if her response was important to him. For a brief moment she couldn't drag her gaze away, and the air between them became increasingly, unexpectedly charged. Skye abruptly pulled her gaze away, clearing her throat as she bought herself a little time. When she felt as if she had something of a grip, she met his gaze again. His expression was cool and businesslike for Tyler, making her half wonder if she'd imagined the crazy edgy vibe between them only seconds before.

"I have an idea," she said, annoyed that her voice was huskier than normal. "You pay for the repairs and we'll get them done right now. I'll manage the day-to-day operations, *and* I'll pay you back as I can."

He nodded his approval. "If we get roofs on those buildings before winter, we won't lose them, but they're in bad shape right now, Skye, and we don't need any more water running down inside of them."

"I know." She leaned back, half wondering if she was trying to put more distance between them. Suddenly, the picnic table didn't seem wide enough anymore. Annoyed at herself, she plopped her forearms on the table and leaned forward.

"As to the cattle—"

"I'll handle the cattle."

Tyler's mouth flattened before he asked in a patient voice, "You have some slick calves. When are you planning to brand?"

"About two weeks."

"I want to be here."

"Why? I've managed quite well without you in the past."

"I'm going to do my share."

"You're paying for the roofs." A stubborn expression settled onto his handsome face, but before he could speak, Skye said, "Cliff and his son help me brand in the fall and the spring. I don't have that many slick calves. We'll preg-check then and arrange to ship the empty cows. It'll all be done in one day." Or maybe two. Cliff didn't like doing everything in one day, but Tyler didn't need to know that. She leaned even closer toward him. "I want carte blanche on the cattle." Something that wasn't in the agreement. Something, judging from his expression, he wasn't going to agree to.

"Until the spring."

"Until the spring," she echoed. She resisted the urge to ask what happened then. She'd take things one day at a time, just as she'd taken them since Mason's death.

A gust of wind blasted over them, lifting and tipping the cinnamon roll pan. Both grabbed for it at the same time, and Skye snatched her hands back as Tyler covered them with his own. He righted the pan, meeting Skye's gaze before she got up and crossed the lawn to pick up the napkins that had blown away. She crumpled them in her hand and headed back to the table, where Tyler was already on his feet.

"You never answered my question," he said.

Skye tipped her chin up. "What question is that?" she asked, knowing full well what he was referring to.

"The one about why we never got along."

She gave a careless shrug. "I don't know...spiders. Snakes. The incessant teasing?" His knack for finding little weaknesses and insecurities and exploiting them. "You were merciless toward me."

"You mean I was acting like a preadolescent boy who liked a girl?"

She stared at him, stunned, as heat flooded her cheeks, which was ridiculous. But ridiculous or not, her cheeks were hot and she didn't know what to say.

Tyler gave a little laugh. "You didn't know?"

"How could I know?"

"I thought I was telegraphing my feelings pretty well back then."

Skye couldn't find words. He'd had a crush on her? "If that was how you showed that you liked someone, then I'd hate to see how you treated someone you didn't like."

"I ignored them." She gave him an uncertain sidelong glance, and he explained, "Our dad taught Jess and I not to waste energy on people who treat you poorly or people you don't particularly like."

"You didn't see what you were doing to me was akin to treating me poorly?"

He gave his head a simple shake, somehow looking sexy as hell as he said, "Nope. I was eleven years old and I was a courtin'."

Skye rolled her eyes as her cheeks warmed, thankful to have something to distract her from the other questions crowding into her head—such as why had he asked her out in high school?

Tyler hooked his thumb in his belt loop. "This isn't going to be easy, is it?"

"I see no way that it can be." Skye spoke truthfully, thankful that he hadn't cued into the direction of her thoughts. "But—" she had to say it "—I appreciate the fact that you've given me a chance to hang on to the ranch." She owed him for that. She might hate it, but the old cliché about beggars not being choosers came into play here.

"Seemed like the thing to do." He spoke without any hint of emotion. "You should know, too, that I'm leaving in two days."

"Will you be back anytime soon?"

"I might squeeze in a day or two—like when you brand—but for the most part, no. I'll be hitting it hard for the next three months." One corner of his mouth twisted in a rather grim smile. "So you'll have your ranch to yourself for the most part. The only person here will be the handyman fixing the roofs and fences."

"Do you blame me for feeling that way, Ty? I've been alone here for a year. Been my own boss forever. It's not easy having someone come in and take charge."

"No, I don't blame you, Skye. But it's something you have to get used to." His expression grew serious. "I didn't make your situation, so I'd kind of appreciate it if I wasn't on the receiving end of your frustration."

She had no defense. She couldn't deny her frustration and anger, and she couldn't deny that she was taking it out on him, even after determining that he was probably not responsible for Mason's gambling.

"Then let me continue to run my ranch."

"Not a problem…for now."

She tilted her chin up. "When might it be a problem?"

"When I'm living on the ranch full-time and want equal say…just like the agreement says I get."

She swallowed and gave a curt nod. She'd sold her soul to save her ranch and now she had to live with the decision. "I foresee future discussions."

"Peaceful ones, I hope."

"When has anything been peaceful between you and me?" The question sounded bitter, and Skye instantly regretted her tone. "Not to say that we can't make things peaceful." There. A save. Kind of.

Tyler's expression shifted and Skye found herself on the receiving end of a long, speculative look. "Do you think that's possible?" His tone was low and surprisingly serious. "I mean…will you allow that to happen?"

"Me?"

"Yes, Skye, you."

She started to speak, although she had no idea what she was about to say, then abruptly stopped. There was nothing worse than your nemesis bringing up a valid point. "I'll do my best," she finally said in a flat voice. "Will you?"

He smiled at her in a way that bordered on predatory, causing a small tremor to move through her midsection. "Yeah. I will, Skye. As I see it, that's the only way we're going to survive this partnership."

TY COULDN'T HELP but wonder if it was a coincidence that Skye worked double shifts at the café for the next two days, leaving early in the morning and coming home just before dark. When she got home, Tyler decided not to be a jerk, since he'd had the place to himself all day, and stayed in his trailer while she fed and cared for her many animals. The first day after completing her feeding chores, she went straight from the barn to the house, but the second day, after shooting a look at his trailer, as if to assure herself that he wasn't watching her, which he was, she crossed the pasture to the fresh grave there and stood for several minutes first staring down at the dirt, then off across the horizon.

Skye had known a lot of loss.

Tyler turned away from the window and walked

down the narrow hall to his bedroom, essentially giving her the privacy she deserved as she mourned her horse. She was never going to like him. He was going to have to get that through his thick skull. Maybe some year she'd loosen up, let him be a friend, but she was never going to be easy with him the way she was easy with his twin.

Just recalling the horrified look on her face when she'd realized that he'd picked on her because of a schoolboy crush hadn't done his ego one bit of good.

Well, fine, Skye. You may not ever like me, but you're going to have to learn to deal with me.

Tyler went back to tossing things into his duffel. He was flying out of Butte the next day for Albuquerque, where the tour kicked off its second leg. After that it was three weeks of travel, a week off, three weeks of travel. He'd head back to the ranch for the week off, see how Skye was faring without him. His mouth twisted at the thought.

She would be doing very well without him, but hey...the ranch was half his, and he was going to spend his downtime there.

Skye was going to have to learn to share.

Tyler left well before daybreak—pulling his truck out of the drive just after she'd gotten out of bed for her early morning shift. They'd spoken briefly the night before after he knocked on her door and offered her the extra key to his trailer in case she needed to get in while he was gone. Skye thanked him and wished him luck.

"When you're good, you don't need luck."

"All bull riders need luck," she'd retorted. No matter

how much skill a rider had, there were circumstances beyond his control. He'd simply raised his hand and headed back down the steps toward his trailer.

Now he was gone. And Skye felt like she could breathe again.

She watched the dust from Tyler's truck die down, then walked down to the barn with Jinx trotting by her side. Her ranch was hers once again...until Tyler came back. She had his schedule tacked to the refrigerator so that she knew exactly where he was and when. If things went well, she wouldn't see much of him until the summer hiatus. She was hoping that he might try to pick up a few summer events, and then he'd be gone even longer.

Probably not a nice way to think about the guy who'd bailed her out, but she couldn't help it. Whether it was fair or not, she couldn't totally shake the idea that Mason would have fared better if he hadn't had wild friends. And Tyler was a wild one.

Well, she could maybe find comfort in the fact that if she went down, she was no longer going down alone. She'd have someone to discuss the matter with.

Yes. She'd grab on to that. She wasn't alone. Mason had been dead for over a year. She'd mourned and she'd fought to keep her ranch. Alone.

Maybe she needed to get out. Make a new life now that the financial burden had been eased and she no longer had to pinch every penny and worry about making that next payment. She was in no way in the clear, but she was better off than she'd been in over a year.

Like it or not, she had Tyler to thank for that.

She did not like.

Chapter Seven

"The big question tonight is can Tyler Hayward do it a third time?" The cheer that went up from the crowd in response to the announcer's question indicated yes, they believed that Tyler could take home the top money three times in a row.

And why not? He'd killed in Albuquerque, having drawn a bull that hadn't been ridden in over six months and just making the buzzer before going off over his hand. Then in Oklahoma City he'd drawn another rank bull and gave a crowd-pleasing eighty-eight-point performance. He'd landed on his feet that time. It didn't happen often, but when it did, there was nothing better.

His draw that day, Bad Carl, a Brahman-Charolais cross, was a big, seemingly sluggish bull with a spotty record. Sometimes he bucked like a dynamo, sometimes he didn't.

"You'd better give it your all today, because I need a score," Ty muttered to the bull, who rolled a dark eye and flicked a buttercream-colored ear at him in response. "Yeah. Right back at you."

Tyler carefully adjusted his grip, then pounded his glove. He shifted his weight, pushing down through his legs and feet, his free hand on the top gate rail as he found the middle. One quick nod and the gate flew open. Bad Carl quivered for a moment, then lunged out of the chute, kicking so high that he was inches away from doing a somersault, and then rearing up to throw Tyler forward and smack him square in the face with the top of his head.

Sparks, brighter than the LED headlights he hated so much, obliterated Tyler's vision. His free hand hit the bull's shoulder, and somewhere in the deep recesses of his brain, he registered that he'd just disqualified himself. But, that didn't matter, because the ground came crashing up at him, then he tasted dirt. The stars disappeared, but with his ear pressed hard against the ground, he could still hear the thunder of hooves hitting all around him. He automatically rolled into a ball as one came close to his back, then tried to get to his feet as the bull moved away, staggering a little. The bullfighter took hold of his left arm and helped him to his feet. He was wobbly, but the crowd cheered and he lifted his hand, only to wince as pain ripped through his right side.

The bullfighter steadied him, and together they walked a few steps, then the bullfighter fell back, allowing Tyler the last several yards under his own steam. As soon as he made it through the man gate, a paramedic escorted him to the medical station.

"Bad Carl lived up to his name tonight," the paramedic said in a cheerful voice as he sat Tyler down.

"From your tone of voice, I gather that I'm not going to die." His head was starting to clear.

"No. But you're going to hurt. You just ripped the hell out of this shoulder."

Tyler squeezed his eyes shut and let his head fall back against the wall. "Ripped. How badly ripped?"

"You did some damage."

Tyler's head throbbed. He'd gone for so long without a debilitating injury that he'd started to feel bulletproof. Never a good thing in bull riding.

"The good news is that you didn't break your nose."

Hard to believe, since he felt as if he'd been hit in the face with a fence post. "Then what's all this?" Tyler pointed at the front of his shirt, which was covered with blood and dirt, and he could still feel the stuff oozing down his face and out of his nose.

"I'd say the gash between your eyebrows."

"Sweet." Tyler tried to pull a breath in through his nose. He failed, and the effort hurt. "You're sure it's not broken?"

"Yeah. Swollen, but not broken."

"Small blessings." He moved his shoulder, winced again. Pain was no stranger to him, but this went beyond pain. The shoulder felt oddly weak. Useless. "You think I'm going to be out for a while?"

The medic stood back. "Talk to the doc, see what he says."

SKYE SIPPED HER coffee and studied the calendar on her refrigerator. She had fourteen days of peace before Tyler returned for a short break. With Cliff's help, she'd managed to get the branding and preg-checking done a few days after his departure, despite Tyler's insistence upon being there to assist. Skye couldn't help it—she felt territorial. Tyler could putter around the ranch to his heart's content as long as he stayed away from her and her cows. There was nothing about that in the agreement, but she was fairly certain she could get her point across without having it in writing. At the very least, they'd discuss the matter.

Yes—they would discuss. Partnership and all that.

Skye set down her coffee cup and gently rolled her neck, taking out the kinks and noting that her muscles weren't nearly as stiff as they'd been not that long ago. As much as she hated to admit it, she'd been sleeping better since Tyler bought into the ranch. She didn't like sharing control of her operation, especially with a man who'd driven her so crazy in the past, but she was no longer overwhelmed by fear of losing everything. For the first time in a long time, Skye felt free to make plans—to act instead of react. She had projects on the ranch that she'd ignored for too long as she struggled to hang on. Now she could tackle some of them.

Now she could build her chicken house.

She'd had chickens as a kid, but they'd roosted in the barn, thus making them easy prey for various nocturnal varmints. After her last hen had gone to the big chicken coop in the sky, she'd decided not to keep chickens until she had a proper house. There hadn't been a hen on the place for almost fifteen years.

It was time.

Jinx threw himself against her legs, and Skye set down her cup to get a kitty treat out of the ceramic container next to the flour and sugar. The cat was spoiled, and she didn't care. He'd been a steady companion during the rough times.

"Fourteen days, Jinxy. Can we get our chicken house done by then?" There was a lot of scrap lumber stored in the barn, but she'd have to buy wire and roofing—or perhaps she could finagle a deal from the roofing crew that had finally shown up the day before.

She wasn't familiar with the outfit—they'd driven over from a nearby town—but they'd given Tyler the best price and had seemed polite and professional as they spent the day ripping into the outbuildings. Tyler was right about the roofs—they should have been replaced years ago and a few more bad winters would destroy the buildings. It was hell keeping up with an aging ranch and even worse to see it falling down around her.

But at least the equipment was new—thank you, Mason. He'd done a good job around the place when he'd been there, even though his heart hadn't totally been into ranching and farming. He'd been a bull rider, pure and simple.

Skye had just poured the last of the coffee into her cup when she heard a truck pull in. The roofers were early. She picked up the cup and headed out to the front porch, only to almost drop it when she stepped outside. Dear heavens, no.

Tyler climbed out of his truck, his movements stiff and awkward. Skye closed her eyes, took a calming breath. He was back. Fourteen days early. That could mean only one thing. He caught sight of her then, gave a curt nod in her direction and headed around the bunkhouse to his trailer.

Skye couldn't help herself. She set down the cup on the porch rail and started down the walk. Tyler came back around the bunkhouse as she reached his truck, and even at a distance she could see that both eyes were black. He seemed startled to see that she'd moved into his territory. She was certainly startled by his appearance, although, having been married to a bull rider, she shouldn't have been. He had four stitches along the bridge of his nose. Both eyes were black. And his nose was swollen and bruised, as was the right side of his face.

"How long are you out for?" she asked flatly.

"Four to six weeks. If I behave myself, I may be able to compete for the rest of the season without surgery."

Skye lifted her eyebrows, unable to squelch the expression of disbelief. None of this was new to her. "Will you be able to hold off for four weeks?" Because she knew it would never be six.

"Going to do my best." He opened the truck door and pulled out his duffel with what must have been his good hand. Judging from the odd way he was moving, his right shoulder was probably bandaged under his shirt.

Four weeks. Four. Long. Weeks.

This is what you signed on for. You can do this.

"I see that the roofing crew showed up," Tyler said as he shut the truck door.

"They got here just before I left for my shift yesterday and were gone when I came home." In that amount of time they'd stripped half the roofing from three buildings, which seemed like an odd way to tackle the project, but Skye figured that as long as they got it done, she didn't care how they did things.

Tyler frowned as he studied the buildings. "I wonder why they aren't here now."

Skye shrugged, even though she'd been wondering the same thing. She had a more pressing question. "Why didn't you let me know you were coming home early?"

He smiled at her, but it was lopsided due to the swelling on the left side of his face. "Planning big parties when I'm not around?"

"Yes. I'm such a party person," she snapped.

"Maybe you should be," he replied easily, making her aware of how waspish she'd just sounded.

"Why is that?" Skye took care not to bite her words out.

Tyler closed the door to the truck, wincing a little as he did so. "If you let go every now and again, you might feel less stress. Right now you're a candidate for a heart attack."

Tyler Hayward was giving her life advice?

"Thanks for the judgment," she said. "Perhaps I should tell you that riding bulls is hazardous to your health. No. Wait. Maybe you already know that, yet you continue, even though it defies logic."

"What's your point, Skye?"

A sigh escaped her lips. "No point. I'm just reacting." As always.

His eyebrows lifted...or at least tried to go up. She was definitely going to have to find a video of his wreck—it had to be a good one given the state of his face.

"I'm not trying to bait you," he said. "I'm just... talking."

Stop being so reasonable. Skye sighed again, inwardly this time, and went with the truth. Partners should be truthful. "Sorry for being short with you. I thought I had two weeks of alone time and didn't expect you back so soon. I'm not used to sharing the place." She resented sharing the place, but she was better off because of it. For now anyway.

"Feel free to go about your business. I'll be passed out in my trailer."

"For the whole four weeks?" she asked innocently.

"I wish," he said, rubbing his shoulder.

"Pain meds?"

"Lack of sleep. I drove most of the night to get here."

For some reason the thought of him driving all night while injured bothered her. It was habit, of course. She was conditioned to worry about bull riders and their crazy ways, but damned if she was going to worry about another bull rider. "Look—"

"Skye. Stop." He met her gaze dead on, all traces of easy humor gone from his face, and the rest of her sentence died on her lips. The blue-and-yellow bruises around his eyes and the stitches between his eyebrows made him look all the more serious as he said, "You don't need to hammer the point home. I understand that you don't want me here."

"Then why are you living here?" she asked in a low voice, even as she told herself to just shut up. "You could have parked your trailer on Jess's property. It isn't that far away."

"Keeping an eye on my investment. Sorry you hate it so much." He gave her a nod before adjusting his grip on his duffel and heading for his trailer, moving stiffly as he crossed the short distance.

Skye watched him go, her mouth tight. If they were going to coexist, she really, *really* had to start thinking before she spoke.

She turned on her heel and headed back to the house. He was back for a goodly amount of time, and she had to deal. She'd still go to work on her chicken house, but she was taking the coward's way out and building it on the opposite side of the barn from Tyler's trailer.

TYLER WOKE WITH a start, then groaned as he pushed himself upright. Bull dream. He didn't have them too often, but every now and again, a bull stomped him good while he slept. He swung his feet onto the floor and sat a minute, waiting for his groggy thoughts to clear before getting to his feet and walking down the short hallway to the kitchen. Outside he could hear the sound of hammering. The roofing crew, no doubt. He'd have to see how it was going and get a time estimate. Once they were done, he was going to slap a fresh coat of paint on the siding—using his good arm, of course. How hard could it be to paint left-handed? Next year they'd tackle the barn, which wasn't in as bad of shape as the rest of the buildings. Mason had not been one for maintenance.

He guessed he could say the same thing for Skye, but she'd worked full-time while Mason had been on the road, pursuing his career, so when would she have had time? If Mason had been dipping into the ranch fund that he'd drained for as long as Tyler suspected, he'd probably discouraged Skye from hiring out any repairs.

Skye…beautiful, closed-off Skye, who had never been closed off with his brother. Tyler was not his brother, and Skye was not the fantasy woman he'd made her out to be…but there was something about her that continued to draw him in, made him feel protective even as she took potshots at him. She was his business partner, who resented him, yet needed him, which probably made her resent him even more. *Great situation, Hayward.* And not one that would be sorted out anytime soon.

Tyler turned on the tap and poured a glass of water, then took a couple of ibuprofen tablets to dull the aches in his shoulder and his head. He caught the sound of distant hammering and decided to check the roofers' progress, hoping the fresh air would help clear his head. He'd driven too far last night before pulling into a truck stop and catching two hours of sleep and then driving again. He wanted nothing more than to be unconscious, but the aches in his body were stronger than the urge to sleep.

The hammering from the other side of the barn stopped as Tyler stepped out of his trailer, and that was when he realized that the driveway was empty. No truck belonging to a roofing crew. The only vehicles were Skye's old ranch truck and her small car. The hammering continued on and off as he crossed the driveway and walked around the barn to the opposite side, where Skye was kneeling over a small two-by-four frame. She was about to swing the hammer again when she heard his footsteps and instead of smacking the nail, laid her hammer down and got to her feet.

"You didn't sleep long," she said, dusting her hands on her jeans and looking more than a little self-conscious. Secret project? "Did the hammering bother you?"

"I thought it was the roofers." As curious as he was, he didn't ask about her project. They'd keep things on business-level, because that was where she wanted them kept and right now he felt too foggy to hold his own.

"They haven't shown." She pushed tendrils of wind-blown hair off her face. "Seems kind of odd." She tilted her chin up as she spoke, and he wondered if she was making an effort not to say anything to start another argument. If so, he truly appreciated it. They could pick up again when he felt more himself.

"Yeah. It does." He checked his watch. Eleven o'clock. "I'll give them a call. See what gives."

"Let me know."

"Yeah. I will." He glanced down at the frame, then turned without comment and headed back to his phone in the trailer.

Skye shot Tyler a cautious look as he came back out of his trailer five minutes later, as if expecting bad news. She would not be disappointed.

"The number is disconnected."

She blinked. "As in…"

"Out of service."

"Maybe a glitch?"

"I have a bad feeling it's not." He looked past her to the roofs that now had no shingles. Roofs in worse shape than they'd been when he'd contracted the job.

"If it's not a glitch…" Her mouth tightened, as if she didn't want to acknowledge the alternative out loud. Neither did Tyler. He had money tied up in this deal—one-third of the cost of the job—and now that he wouldn't be riding for the next four weeks, this could turn out to be some serious stuff.

"I'd better go to town. See what's going on." She gave him a sideways glance, her gaze traveling over his banged-up shoulder in a speaking way. "Hey," he said. "It isn't like I didn't just drive seven hundred miles to get here from Reno."

"I'm coming with you." When he lifted his chin, she

met his eyes, a vaguely challenging light in her own. "Partners, remember?"

Twenty minutes later he pulled his truck to a stop in front of the building where he'd made the deal to roof the outbuildings. The windows were dark, the small parking lot was empty and there was an ominous-looking bright pink sign on the door.

"Not good," Skye muttered, reaching for her door handle.

No. Not good at all.

They came around their respective sides of the truck to walk together to the abandoned office to read the notice. Tyler stopped a few sentences after "Out of Business," but Skye leaned closer to read the rest of the smaller print.

When she was done she looked over at Tyler. "How much of your money do they have?"

"A couple grand."

She exhaled. "I have a feeling that we're going to be in a long line of creditors if they shut down just like this. How much research did you do before booking these guys?"

"Research?" He frowned at her. "I asked places for bids. These guys came in lowest."

"Did you check online reviews?"

"I don't see where reviews would have warned me that these guys were about to secretly go out of business."

"True."

He studied the Out of Business sign grimly. "They knew they were going out of business and they took my money."

"That stinks."

Tyler shot Skye a quick look and decided that she wasn't being sarcastic. He pushed his hands into his jacket pockets. "What stinks even more is that we have half roofs on all of the buildings." That and the fact that he felt stupid for dealing with these guys. The price they'd given him was so much lower than the lumberyard in Gavin that maybe he should have suspected something was up. Shaking his head, he headed back to the truck.

"What now?" Skye asked as she caught up with him.

"I buy shingles and do what these guys were supposed to do."

"You?"

She may not have meant to sound insulting, but all the same… "I'm not without skills."

"Have you ever roofed anything—?"

He scowled at her. "It's not rocket science."

"While incapacitated?" she continued smoothly, ignoring his interruption.

"Incapacitated?" He gave a scoffing laugh. "Nothing's broken."

"Which hand is your hammer hand?"

"So I learn to hammer left-handed. Big deal."

"Jarring your shoulder every time you take a swing? Yes. That will help your recovery."

He had a strong feeling that she was concerned about his recovery only because the sooner he recovered, the sooner he would be out on the road again. "What do you suggest?" he asked with exaggerated patience.

Her mouth flattened and she started for her side of the truck. "Let's go price shingles." She yanked the door open. "And we better start buying the newspaper, in case there's a notice of bankruptcy. Or maybe we can sue in small claims court."

"Yeah." But for all intents and purposes, the money was gone and he needed to focus on getting roofs on the buildings. "I'll see if Jess is available to help with the roofs."

She put the truck into Reverse, and an odd grinding sound came out of the transmission. He looked over at her with a questioning raise of his eyebrows. "Ignore it," she said as she shifted into a forward gear.

"I don't know how long you can ignore stuff like that before it gets you into trouble."

"I'll take my chances."

"I don't want you stranded somewhere."

"I don't go anywhere," she pointed out. "I go to work and I go home. Sometimes I go shopping in town on a day off. It isn't as if I'm heading out across the wilds of Montana." She checked for traffic, then eased out onto the road. "Besides, I couldn't afford to get it fixed if I wanted to."

"It will need fixed."

"Right now I'm more concerned about the roofs." She kept her gaze glued to the road, but he saw the corner of her mouth go tight. "If you're out of work for a while—"

"I still have some money." Enough to buy roofing and fencing anyway.

"But we're making a plan before we act. Right?"

"Oh, no way. Why make plans when you can shoot from the hip and compound your mistakes? I'm all about the impulse."

She shot him a dry look. "I figured."

"Here's the thing, Skye—we need to fix the roofs before the weather starts. I say we buy enough stuff to start now and plan later."

"Any idea what we need?"

"Tar paper. Shingles. Nails." A bunch of money. "I'll put it on my credit card until I can access my savings account."

"I don't know…"

"I do. We need to roof those buildings soon."

She put her hand on the edge of the door, narrowing her eyes at him. "Just so we're straight on this, when I eventually pay off the mortgage—" and he could see by her expression that she had every intention of doing that "—I reimburse you for the repairs. Are you keeping track? Or am I?"

"Half the repairs."

"Is that what the contract says?"

"That's what I say."

"That would give you a continued stake in the ranch."

"Don't worry, Skye—you'll eventually get the place free and clear."

She opened her mouth as if to argue, then seemed to think better of it…as in, she'd fight this battle at a better time than while sitting in a truck in the parking lot of the expensive lumberyard.

"I'll keep track," she said. "And maybe you'd better also keep track, to keep me honest."

"I'm not exactly worried about your honesty, Skye."

She shrugged nonchalantly as they walked toward the door. "You never know. I may be an accomplished liar."

Tyler managed a small smile, but his mouth hardened as soon as she looked away. No. She was not the accomplished liar. Mason had been.

Chapter Eight

Skye did some online research as Tyler spoke with a sales associate at the lumberyard. He was right—they had to deal with this mini-disaster as soon as possible, and if the prices here were close to those at the big-box stores in Bozeman, then they'd buy today. If not, then she voted for taking their chances with the weather. Years of frugality were not easily set aside—especially when her business partner was out of a job for at least a month—probably more if he insisted on hammering. Maybe he wouldn't do that. Bull riders lived to ride—although they had an unrealistic sense of what they were capable of. Ride with a broken leg? Why not? Two broken feet? Go for it.

Hammering shingles on a roof? Child's play.

Tyler and Mason were so very similar in that regard that it made her wonder if Tyler would finish the roofs before deciding he was well enough to go back on tour. Mason had started several projects—fence repairs, flooring repairs, corral cleanups—only to abandon them out of necessity and lack of time when he headed back out on tour to earn his living. But roofs were different. Roofs were necessary.

Tyler appeared at the end of the aisle and motioned

with his head for her to join him. She'd almost reached him when someone from behind her called his name, and she turned to see Paige Andrews approaching, looking as poised and confident as she had every day of high school, where she'd been student body president and the top scorer on the basketball team. She had a few debating and track honors, too. Paige was an achiever and she liked to be in charge, which worked out well, because she was very good at being in charge.

She came to a stop and smiled at Skye before getting a good look at Tyler's face and wincing.

"Been practicing your craft, I see," she said. Tyler's bruises were blooming, the black turning to blue and the blue to yellow. He looked like a Technicolor raccoon. And, interestingly, Skye noticed color rising in the nonbruised parts of his face as Paige studied him, a faint frown drawing her perfect eyebrows closer together.

"Some days are better than others," Tyler muttered.

"Bull riding is a crazy occupation." Paige gave her head a small shake.

"Pays the bills."

Skye noted that Tyler, who had the social thing down pat, didn't sound all that friendly. Who wasn't friendly to Paige?

The woman cast a glance in Skye's direction. "So you guys are out shopping together?" The unspoken question was obvious. Were they together?

"We're partners," Tyler said before Skye could answer.

"Partners?" Now Paige's eyebrows went up. "In the business sense?"

"Yes." Skye wanted to get that straight immediately, before the rumors started.

"What kind of business?" Paige seemed truly interested, and not in a gossipy sort of way.

"Ranching," Skye said simply.

"Ah." She eased her expensive leather bag off from her shoulder. "I just moved back from Dillon and I'm opening an accounting firm here in Gavin. If you need a ranch accountant—" she pulled a card out of a side pocket of her bag and held it out to Skye "—give me a call."

"Will do."

Tyler gave a curt nod, and Skye began to wonder just what the history was between these two. He might not be Paige's type—she'd always gone for the clean-cut-jock types—but he was gorgeous when he wasn't all beat up.

Although…yeah…Skye had to admit that he had a strong physical appeal even when he *was* beat up. He was a beautiful man, but she found wolves and cougars beautiful, too—that didn't mean she wanted to get close to them. Skye knew trouble when she saw it, and she had recognized Tyler as trouble from the tender age of eleven.

"I need to run," Paige said with an apologetic smile. "I hope to see you again sometime."

Paige walked toward the exit, and Skye felt a brief moment of envy as she watched her go. What would it be like to have things so together? When she looked at Tyler, she found him studying her with an odd expression, and she had no idea why. "What?" she asked, figuring if she challenged him, he wouldn't ask any questions. She was right.

"Nothing." He frowned and headed toward the counter, where the guy manning the register did a double take when he saw Tyler's black eyes and stitches.

"I ran into a door," Tyler muttered. "And I need to price shingles."

ONCE THEY GOT HOME, Skye helped Tyler unload the heavy bundles of shingles, dragging them off the bed of the truck into a stack, Tyler doing as much with one arm as she was doing with two. And while Skye knew better than to point out that he was pushing himself too much, she could think it…then remind herself that it was none of her business. She wasn't married to Tyler. She didn't need to keep him from hurting himself. But that didn't mean she didn't have questions.

"How are we going to get these onto the roof?" Because there was no way either of them could carry a bundle of the heavy, unwieldy shingles up a ladder. "A few at a time?" Which meant trip after trip after trip.

"I called Jess while you were in the house. He'll be here tomorrow."

"That's a relief. We'll pay him, right?"

"He's my brother. He'll get paid—it just may not be in cash."

Skye decided to let that one go, even though it meant being beholden to yet another Hayward. She pulled the tape measure out of her pocket and started measuring the dimensions of the buildings, jotting numbers in a small notebook as she took them, so that she could calculate areas and determine how many more shingles they needed to buy.

She was just starting to measure the granary when

she glanced up to see Tyler studying her with an odd frown. "What?"

"You're making me think that math really can be used in real life."

"Funny."

"Want me to hold the other end of the tape?"

She couldn't help the surprised look on her face. "I got it."

"You don't need to do everything alone, Skye."

She gave a small sniff as she snaked the tape out. "I'm used to it."

"The point is that you don't have to do everything alone."

She met his eyes then. Intense eyes surrounded by angry black bruising. "I'm not a twin."

"What does that have to do with anything?"

"You've always done things together. I'm an only."

Tyler let out a breath as he propped his hands on his hips. "Did you do everything alone when Mason was home?"

"Of course not." *Not much anyway...*

Tyler's eyes narrowed as if he'd just read something in her response that he hadn't expected—which meant she needed to work on her game face.

"He had his responsibilities and I had mine."

"Ah."

"Don't judge what you don't know about, Tyler."

"I'm not judging."

"I think you are."

"Because it's easiest to think the worst of me?" he asked, his easy tone of voice belying the hard look in his eye.

Do not react. Think first. Skye glanced down, took

her time jotting down the final measurement, then pushed the button to rewind the tape into its case. She hooked the tape onto her belt, carefully stowed the notebook in her pocket, then ruined the effect of total self-control by fumbling the pencil. It dropped to the ground and rolled to Tyler's boot. He bent down with a small grimace, telling her just how sore he was, and picked it up. He solemnly held it out, and Skye just as solemnly took it.

"I'm not trying to think the worst of you." She squeezed the pencil so hard that she was surprised it didn't snap.

"It just keeps happening automatically?"

She let out a sigh. "You rescued me. I owe you."

"That doesn't help matters, does it?"

She had to be honest. "No."

The word was barely out of her mouth when a blast of warm wind came out of nowhere, swirling around them. They simultaneously hunched their shoulders, stepping together as the moving air whipped their coats. Seconds later it was gone.

"Storm's moving fast," Tyler said, scanning the dark clouds on the south horizon.

"I have tarps." She started for the barn, not waiting to see if he'd follow, which of course he did. The tarps were old and covered with thick, choking dust. They worked together to drag them out of the barn, ignoring the hissing of her goose, who took exception to Tyler, a stranger, coming close to her sanctuary on the straw stack. Once outside they shook off the dust, both of them coughing as the dust rose around them, then hauled the first tarp to the granary and covered the grain inside, weighting down the old canvas with sledgehammers, bars and picks that Tyler brought from the toolshed nearby.

"I vote for roofing this building first," Tyler muttered.

"Yeah."

They went back for the other tarp and arranged it inside the toolshed. Tyler opened the door of the third half-roofed building, the tack shed, and shook his head. Without waiting for him to speak, Skye said, "Yes. We should move them."

Realizing that she'd just answered a question that hadn't been asked, Skye felt an odd rush of emotion. The only other person she'd ever done that with was Mason.

It was just a fluke. The question had been an obvious one. Skye stalked into the tack room and started pulling bridles off hooks and hanging them over the horn of the nearest saddle. She threw a couple of pads on top and hefted the saddle, edging past Tyler, who was doing the same, and headed toward the door.

The rain started as she started up the walk. She dumped the saddle in her living room and headed back for the next load. Three saddles later, her living room was full of tack and all that was left in the shed were the ropes and halters and grooming equipment—things that could get wet without major consequences.

Tyler dumped his load onto the floor just as the rain started hammering on the roof. He went to the door and pushed it closed.

"Need some help arranging this?"

Since her instinct was to say no, and she knew Tyler fully expected her to say no, Skye said, "Yes. Thank you."

Silently they carried the saddles to the edge of the

room, tipping them up so the skirts didn't curl and draping the blankets and pads over them. Skye brought in a laundry basket, and they filled it with bridles and breast collars.

"Lot of tack," Tyler said when they were done.

"A lot of it was my dad's," Skye replied. They stood side by side, studying the basket, because it was too unsettling to focus on one another—on her end anyway. She had no idea what Tyler felt, but an uncomfortable vibe was once again filling the space between them.

"I noticed that your slick calves have brands."

"They do," Skye agreed. Because they were her calves.

"I thought we were going to brand when I got back on break."

"I decided to do it earlier."

Her stubborn words hung in the air, but Tyler didn't engage. "Next year we'll make a schedule."

And there it was. Another glimpse of that reasonable side of him that kind of reminded her of his brother. She didn't want him to remind her of anyone she liked. She wanted to continue their safe, adversarial relationship. She gave a small sniff. "That makes sense."

His lips curved slightly, as if he knew how difficult it was to make that answer when she wanted to argue with him—to drive a nice deep wedge between them—then to her shock and amazement, he reached up and gently brushed his fingers over the side of her face. She went still as shock rippled through her, then she jerked back.

His hand dropped loosely to his side. "Your cheek is covered with dirt from the tarps."

"Oh." The word choked out as her hand went to her face. "I can get it."

"Yeah." His mouth tightened. "I'd better go."

Oh, yes. He needed to go. Because she could still feel the sensation of his hand brushing across her face, and worse than that, she felt herself reacting to his touch in a very unexpected way.

SMOOTH MOVE, HAYWARD.

Tyler shook his head as he walked through the rain to his trailer. What had he been thinking, touching Skye like that when she'd made it so very clear that she wanted no part of it?

He hadn't been thinking. He'd been acting on instinct. He wouldn't be doing that again.

The low-lying clouds made his small living room darker than usual, but Tyler didn't bother with the lights. Gray day, gray mood. He ate some leftover chicken, stared out the window, paced the short length of the hall. Finally, he made a quick call to his brother, then grabbed his hat and headed for the door. A little Shamrock time would lighten his mood, and he could bribe his brother into helping him with the roofs in exchange for…something.

It was almost dark by the time he parked behind the bar, which was nearly empty. Apparently nobody felt like coming out in the rain on a weeknight, but he was glad to be out of his trailer, off the ranch.

"You're a wreck," Jess said as he offered Tyler a chair by shoving it away from the table with his foot.

"It looks worse than it is." And it wasn't as if it was the first time he'd had a couple of black eyes and stitches, although this was the first time he'd had the two together.

"More like it could have been worse than it is."

"That, too." After hitting the ground, there was always that pregnant pause as the fates decided whether or not a bull rider was going to be kicked, crunched, stepped on or rolled.

"How's ranch life?"

Tyler tried to raise an eyebrow, but it didn't go too far. "Skye's not happy to have me back."

"Did you think she would be?"

Tyler pulled the beer his brother had waiting for him closer, but he didn't drink. "I got scammed by a roofing company. Now three of her outbuildings have half roofs and I have to finish them." He met Jess's gaze. "I could use some help. Will you be around?"

"Unfortunately, yes."

"Unfortunately?"

"I was supposed to have a job in Billings, putting up a big-ass metal building, but we're on the verge of losing the contract."

"Sorry to hear that. Maybe it's a sign."

Jess gave him a humorless smile. "You're not going to be happy until I'm as ugly as you are."

"I'm not going to be happy until you use your talents before you're too old to do so." He wouldn't encourage his brother to try for the tour if it wasn't for the fact that he knew that Jess loved the challenge of bull riding as much, if not more, than he did. But that cautious, build-a-stable-life thing always got the better of him. Being a decent brother, he didn't point out that the build-a-stable-life thing didn't seem to be working out all that well.

"It's supposed to rain on and off all week."

"And then there may be an early snow. I've been watching the forecast." He finally took a drink. "Will you help me?"

"Happy to." Jess smiled his then-you'll-owe-me smile.

They fell into silence, then Jess asked him about his shoulder and Tyler gave him the details—finish the season, consult with his doctor about surgery, hope for a full and rapid recovery so he didn't miss too much of the following season.

Jess soaked it all in, but Tyler had the feeling that he was also gnawing on another matter as he listened. Finally, Tyler said, "What?"

"You said Skye wasn't happy to see you."

"Yeah?"

Jess settled his forearms on the table. "Why did you move onto the ranch?"

"Because if either of us had gained an ounce of weight, we wouldn't have fit into your camp trailer."

Jess shook his head. He wasn't buying. Fine. "To keep an eye on my investment. Be a partner."

"And Skye was good with that?" Before Tyler could answer, Jess went on to ask, "Or was she in a position where she didn't have a lot of choices?"

"Are you saying I took advantage?"

"I'm asking about your motivation and goals."

One thing about it…a guy didn't need a conscience if he had a twin like Jess. "My motivation was to keep Skye from losing the ranch."

"Okay."

"And to invest my money."

"All right."

"I hadn't planned on being there all that often. You know that I'm gone more than I'm home." Jess didn't answer. Tyler pushed his beer glass back and forth between his hands, then raised his eye to meet his twin's gaze. "I'm not going to admit to unrequited love, if that's what you're waiting for."

"You don't know her well enough for that."

True, but he'd always felt that connection…and a couple of times recently, he'd thought that she might have felt it, too. Of course, she'd always seemed a little horrified afterward, which wasn't exactly promising.

He pulled in a deep breath and leaned back in his chair, dropping an arm over the back. "I've always cared for Skye. You know that. But she also made me mad by making out as if I was getting Mason out of bed and marching him to the blackjack tables."

"And by marrying Mason."

Tyler clamped his mouth shut. There was a limit to how much he would admit to. "I didn't save her ranch for revenge. I honestly needed an investment. And I… wanted to help her."

"Then give her a break."

"I'm trying." The words snapped out. "She's pretty much fighting me on everything."

"She feels powerless."

So did he in a lot of ways.

Tyler let out a breath and focused on his beer. Apparently he'd shared the womb with a psychologist. He took a long drink, draining a good part of the glass, then set it down carefully. "Here's the deal," he said. "Skye would have lost the ranch if it hadn't been for me. She agreed to this partnership, and I'm going to be an active partner, as *agreed*." He smiled darkly. "You can drop by every now and then so that she can vent about me doing what we agreed upon."

Jess shook his head instead of responding. "When do you want to start roofing?"

"Tomorrow."

"Unless I get an eleventh-hour call from my boss, I'll be there at eight or nine."

"Great. I appreciate it." Tyler drained his glass. "One more thing."

"Yeah?"

"I don't want to talk about Skye anymore."

A FEW DAYS ago she had roofs. Now she had sieves.

Skye paced through her living room, occasionally glancing out the window toward the county road. Tyler had headed off to town hours ago, leaving her in precious peace, except that Skye found she couldn't relax. Not when she knew he was coming back.

The character of the ranch had changed over the past few days. It was no longer her sanctuary, the place where she could hole up and let the world go by. The place where she could recharge after a day of dealing with people. Now, when she should be recharging, she was seething instead. And waiting for his inevitable return.

Skye pushed her hair back from her forehead with both hands. This was her reality, and only she could control the way she reacted to it. Jinx had not gone out that night, perhaps sensing that she needed both a snuggle buddy and an ally. Now he butted his head against her chin, insisting in his feline way that she chill.

She dropped a hand onto his back and stroked. The big cat's motor started, and Skye closed her eyes. At some point she dropped off, because when the throb of the diesel engine jerked her awake, her thighs were almost numb from the weight of the heavy cat. Her partner and adversary was home. Skye nudged Jinx off her lap and stood, shaking out her tingling limbs, then jumping a mile when the first footstep hit her porch. A moment later there was a knock on the door.

Skye checked the porch through the side window. Sure enough, it was Tyler.

Why?

She jerked open the door, did her best not to glare up at her business partner who'd woken her up.

"Your donkey is out. He won't let me near him."

Skye rolled her eyes, then reached for her coat. At least it wasn't raining. "Thank you. I've been meaning to string a lower wire, so he doesn't escape so easily, but he's been staying in lately."

Skye headed off across the drive to where she could see Chester standing on the opposite side of the fence from Babe, which explained why the mule had been so silent. Tyler hadn't followed her, so she took her time getting a halter out of the barn and catching the donkey. She put him back into the corral with Babe, then noticed that the sunflower patch near the barn had been decimated. That explained the escape. Chester would be on reduced rations the next day.

As she started back across the drive, she slowed as she saw that Tyler was waiting for her at the end of her walk.

"Thanks for the heads-up," she said.

"He probably would have been okay until morning, but like I said, your light was on."

"I fell asleep in the chair."

He gave a short nod, the light filtering out of the living room window accentuating his cheekbones. Even beaten up and swollen, his face was something. He was more handsome than Mason had been, and judging from his breath, just as fond of beer.

"Jess is coming to help me with the roofs tomorrow."

"Good to know."

An awkward silence settled between them—one in which it was obvious that he had things to say, but for some reason wasn't. Finally he gave her a single nod of dismissal and brushed past her, disappearing around the bunkhouse. She heard the trailer door open and then close, but she didn't move.

She hated how unsettled she felt around him. Hated that he could, just by knocking on her door and telling her that her escape-artist donkey was out, boost her adrenaline to the point that she didn't know if she'd be able to fall asleep again.

"I CANNOT UNDERSTAND why Paige Andrews and Tiffani Crenshaw are still friends," Angie said as the two women left the café after an early lunch. "It isn't like Tiffani cares much about anything except for Tiffani. Surely Paige has figured that out by now."

Indeed, the hair salon owner did have a reputation for being both self-centered and way too interested in the goings-on of everyone else in the community, but Angie also had a similar rep. She wasn't self-centered, but she was a gossip extraordinaire.

"Opposites attract?" Skye asked. And even though it was none of her business, she also wondered what the deal was with Paige and Tyler. Judging from the encounter in the ranch supply store, they'd been more than passing acquaintances, and even though it bordered on being irrational, given their situation, Skye couldn't say that she liked the idea of the two of them together. For Paige's sake, of course.

"Maybe." Angie looked unconvinced, but since she and Tiffani had had a few skirmishes over the years, Angie was predisposed to disliking the woman. "I thought that Paige would have figured out Tiffani by now."

"She might have figured her out a long time ago and accepted her as she is."

Angie made a face at Skye. "Do you have to keep being positive when I'm trying so hard to be negative?"

Skye laughed. "Sorry. I'll watch myself."

"At least they tip well," Angie muttered as she put bills into the tip jar. She looked over her shoulder. "I'm sure it was Paige."

Skye just smiled again and then headed out from behind the counter as a couple she didn't know came in through the door. She guided them to seats and set the menus on the table.

"Is the weather here always like this in the summer?" the man asked, sounding disappointed.

Skye bent to look out the window. The sky was overcast. Gloomy. "Sometimes, but we have our share of sunny days." Unfortunately, the forecast called for rain on and off for the next several days, but she didn't see any sense in passing that information along. "Where are you visiting from?"

"Alabama."

"You know," the wife muttered, wrapping her sweater around her a little tighter, "where it's warm."

"I've always wanted to visit Alabama," Skye said as

she poured water. "And I hope you have some sunny days while you're here."

The woman picked up her menu with a shake of her head, as if that was never going to happen, and her husband rolled his eyes at her before picking up his menu.

"Unhappy about the weather," she murmured to Angie as she went by.

"Well...it is Montana..."

"Shh."

It didn't rain, but the wind gusted so hard on Skye's drive home that she had to fight to keep her little car on the road at times. When she pulled into her driveway, there was no sign of Jess's truck, which meant the twins must have had the good sense not to try to work in this weather.

The sound of rapid hammering brought her eyes up, and she caught sight of Tyler on the opposite side of the granary roof. Okay. So much for good sense. A wind gust smacked into Skye, nearly knocking her off her feet.

Swallowing a sigh, she headed toward the far side of the granary, hoping to get there before the wind blew Tyler off the roof. If he hurt himself again, he may never leave the ranch.

Chapter Nine

"What are you doing up there?" Skye called when she reached the base of the ladder.

Tyler paused midswing and glanced down as if surprised to see her. "Learning to hammer left-handed." The wind was blowing so strongly that it was difficult to hear him.

Skye put a hand on her forehead to keep her hair out of her eyes. "Where is your brother?"

"On the other side of Montana. He got called out on a job."

"So you've been up there all day?" Obviously from the amount of work he'd gotten done. "Alone?"

"This needs done," he said.

Skye agreed. It did need done. "I have to change."

She turned and headed for the house. He might have called her name—it was difficult to tell over the wind—but she kept walking. Jinx came trotting out from under the porch, and she scooped him up and carried him into the house under one arm. Once inside, she set the heavy cat onto the arm of the sofa, then walked down the hall to her bedroom to change into jeans, running shoes and a sweatshirt. She took a few minutes to rebraid her hair, to keep it from beating her to death, then grabbed gloves out of the basket by the door and headed back out into the weather.

Tyler was coming down off the roof as she rounded the corner of the granary, climbing down the ladder one-handed and making Skye wish that she owned a more stable ladder. Hers was old and wooden and had a couple of loose rungs. In other words, it was an accident waiting to happen and Tyler had been using it all day—with a bum shoulder. Maybe it was because she'd lost her husband not all that long ago to a senseless accident that she was more focused on the possibility of danger than she used to be. Whatever the cause, she felt a flash of annoyance.

"What if you had fallen today?" she asked as soon as Tyler's boots hit the ground.

He frowned at her. "What if you hit a deer with your car while driving home?"

"Meaning?"

"Meaning," he said in a patient voice, "that just because something *can* happen, it doesn't mean that it will."

"So let's just tempt fate?"

He shook his head and then picked up a few sheets of shingles and draped them over his good shoulder. "I tempt fate for a living, sweetheart."

She knew he was being sarcastic, playing the cocky bull rider, but she couldn't help the way her spine stiffened. "Don't call me that."

"Sorry. That was a jerk move." He spoke with a sincerity that almost undid her. He hadn't intended to insult her.

She clenched her teeth for a moment, wondering if she was being unreasonable about not wanting him on a roof with a bad ladder and an injury. No. She wasn't. But he was a bull rider and looked at life differently than normal people. As for the "sweetheart"...

One corner of her mouth quirked as she muttered, "I get called sweetheart a lot at work. Along with honey, dearie, sweetie." She crossed her arms over her chest. "One guy calls me sweet cheeks, and I don't think he's talking about my face."

"Who calls you that?"

There was a note in Tyler's voice that made Skye decide that said guy should remain anonymous. "It doesn't matter. I can deal with it."

He gave her an if-you-say-so look and started up the ladder. The first big fat drops of rain hit just as he dropped the shingles.

"You better come down." The rain would make the roof slick, and it wasn't as if he could finish enough to keep the interior of the shed from getting wet.

"When I finish this row."

There was an open toolbox sitting at the base of the ladder. Skye went over to it, picked up the hammer sitting on top of the tools and closed the lid, then draped four shingles over her shoulder the same way he had. She'd barely started up the ladder when Tyler's face appeared.

"What are you doing, Skye?"

She held up the hammer and continued to climb.

"This roof is going to get slippery," he warned.

"Exactly. So I'll help you get done." She kept climbing. When she scrambled off the ladder onto the new shingles, Tyler frowned at her.

"Be sensible."

Skye laughed. She couldn't help herself. "Really?"

The rain was coming faster now. Tyler shifted his weight, and Skye could plainly see bull rider stubbornness battling logic.

His mouth tightened, then he picked up his hammer and the can of nails, before gesturing to the ladder. "Ladies first." He knelt down to take hold of one of the uprights while she eased herself onto the rungs. The ladder was already slippery, and she was glad to be heading toward earth—and she was glad that Tyler was coming down right after her. She held the ladder until he was halfway down, then stepped back just as his feet came off the rung and he plummeted earthward, grabbing wildly at the ladder, which Skye instantly took hold of.

The hammer missed her, but the nail can hit her on the shoulder as Tyler slid by, landing on his side in the wet gravel at her feet. Skye gasped and dropped to her knees as he pushed himself to a sitting position, pressing his palm against his chin. Blood flowed from between his fingers, dripping on his jeans.

Skye took hold of his fingers and pulled his hand away from his chin, wrinkling her nose as blood ran down his shirt. She instantly pushed his hand back up against his chin. Their faces were close enough that she could see that his pupils had dilated. Pain? Awareness?

Because despite the rain and the blood and the muck, he was studying her in a way that made her pulse bump higher. That was when she realized that she had a hand resting on his knee. Quickly she snatched it away and sat back. Even with another foot of space between them, she could still smell him—wet wool, denim and leather. Man.

"You might need a stitch there," she said as she got

to her feet. She hesitated then held out a hand, because that was what she would do for someone who wasn't making her insides turn small somersaults.

Crazy, crazy, crazy.

But she hadn't been with a guy in a while. Or even around a guy. Plus, Tyler was off-limits. Her business partner. Her former enemy. Forbidden fruit.

Although *enemy* was a strong word. *Nemesis* was better.

"Stitches are for sissies," he said, and Skye felt a bubble of laughter start to rise as she zeroed in on the stitches between his eyes. Great. On top of everything she was becoming hysterical. "I have some butterflies in my med kit," he said.

"Want help?" The last thing she wanted was to be in close quarters with him, touching him, but she was his partner and he was hurt.

"I'm good."

"I'm not squeamish. I've stitched up animals." Her father had taught her how.

He gave her a dark look. "You aren't offering to stitch me up, are you?"

"Maybe your mouth." He choked back a laugh, then grimaced, obviously in pain. Skye wrinkled her nose. "Go take care of that before I do. I'll get the tools out of the rain."

Tyler didn't argue. He turned and started for his trailer, and Skye watched him go for a second, before gathering the nails into the can and then stowing the tools in the barn. She was soaked by the time she was done, but there was still the feeding to do...or there should have been the feeding to do.

All the mangers were full. Even Vanessa the goose's troughs had been filled.

Tyler had fed the menagerie before she could. It made sense, since he'd been home and she'd been at work, but feeding was her time to connect with her animals, and she missed her evening ritual.

Both Chester and Babe were in one small stall that opened out onto the pasture. It was such tight quarters that the mini-donkey was practically standing underneath the tall mule as he ate. Skye noted that neither seemed to care who had fed them. The manger was full, and they were happy.

The rain had stopped by the time she left the barn, but there were so many puddles that Skye had to choose a path between them on the way back to her house. The lights were on in Tyler's trailer, shining golden yellow against the gray day, making Skye wonder how he was doing fixing up his chin. Tyler had to be a pro at doctoring himself up, meaning he'd do fine without her help. And maybe he'd stay off slippery roofs and ladders.

She'd just closed her front yard gate when she heard Tyler's trailer door open and the sound of his boots hitting the ground outside the door. Curious as to where he was going, she waited until he rounded the corner, holding a wadded-up washcloth to his chin.

"Hey," he said as he caught sight of her. "Do you have manicure scissors?"

Skye grimaced at the cloth, which was soaking up blood, before meeting his gaze. "In the mood for a mani-pedi?"

He didn't smile, but she had a feeling he wanted to.

"I want to take the stitches out of my forehead when I get done with my chin. It's time."

"Yes, I have sharp scissors."

"I'm also having a time finding my butterfly sutures. They might be in my truck."

"Or you used them all up the last time you split your face open." She gestured with her head toward her door. "Come on."

Why are you doing this?

No good answer sprung to mind. Maybe because it was the decent thing to do. Maybe to prove to herself that she could be near Tyler and maintain composure. Trial by fire, and all of that. She was going to have to get used to being around the guy—right?

"You have adhesive sutures?" Tyler let himself in through the gate and followed her to the porch.

"Was I married to a bull rider?"

He snorted in reply and Skye assumed that he caught her meaning. Blood and stitches were a way of life.

Skye led Tyler through her house and made him sit in a kitchen chair while she got the scissors, tweezers, gauze, butterfly adhesives and antiseptic cream. If it had been Mason, she'd have sat him down on the commode, but Tyler didn't need to see her newly washed lace bras hanging from the shower rod, or her makeup spread over the counter. Now that the bathroom was hers and hers alone, she left her stuff out where it was handy to get at. And she hung unmentionables wherever she so pleased.

Skye returned to the kitchen to put the supplies on the table along with a two-sided mirror on a stand.

Skye started peeling the covering off the adhesive suture, then handed it to Tyler after he'd wiped his chin clean with a paper towel. She had to admit to being impressed with the way that he quickly pulled the edges of the wound together and applied the butterfly.

"You need another."

"Probably," he agreed as he took the second suture from her. "I know this isn't as much fun for you as sticking me with a needle."

"I'm certain I'll get my chance."

"Looking forward to that?" he asked mildly.

She smiled a little. "You better believe it."

He reached out and picked up the scissors and then leaned toward the mirror to slip the tiny blade under the first stitch and snip. "Tweezers?"

Skye handed them to him and he pulled the first stitch. Skye was no stranger to stitches. She'd been raised around animals and she'd married a bull rider. She retrieved the small trash can from under the kitchen sink without a word and held it out for Tyler to drop the suture into. He gathered up the butterfly wrappers and dropped them in before tackling the second stitch.

Skye watched him work, standing close enough that she could see her reflection in the mirror and was glad that her expression rivaled that of a surgical nurse. Cool and impassive, as if her nerves weren't dancing, and as if she weren't on high alert.

After removing the last suture, Tyler met her eyes in the mirror and Skye suddenly felt as if she were standing a little too close to him, even though she was a good eighteen inches away.

"So what do you think?"

"About...?" she asked coolly.

"Am I pretty again?"

Skye forced a frown, because yes, he did look prettier, and she didn't want to notice those things about her ranch partner. "I'm sure the ladies of Gavin will think so."

He held her gaze for another split second before gathering the items she'd supplied him into a neat pile and getting up from the chair. And that was when Skye's theory that she might be standing too close to him became hard fact. She was too close now, but she wasn't going to move. Tripping over herself to put distance between them wasn't going to make her feel better.

"Thank you for the help."

"I don't think I did that much."

"Never underestimate the value of moral support."

She gave a small snort through her nose. "That's me. Ms. Moral Support."

Heaven knew that had been her role with Mason. One she missed…just as she missed being supported by her husband. They'd had a decent partnership and there were days when she was so tired of fighting the world alone that she felt like curling up and hiding. But that wasn't possible. The world was there, whether she hid or not, so that meant that she needed to face things head-on. Things like this ridiculously attractive man standing way too close to her in her own kitchen, making her feel all jumpy and aware.

He raised his chin, looking down at her from his superior height and Skye fought the urge to tilt her chin up to meet his gaze…mainly because that would bring her lips all the closer to his and she had no business—absolutely no business—wondering how he kissed.

Such thoughts were crazy and dangerous and not

allowed into her head. And if she couldn't get the thoughts out of her head, she needed to get Tyler out of her house. She'd underestimated the impact of having him there.

Tyler cleared his throat. "I'll let you be."

Without waiting for her to reply, he turned and headed toward the door, leaving Skye staring after him. Had he read her thoughts or something?

Or had he felt that same thing she had?

THE GROUND WAS moist and the grass squishy the next morning when Tyler came out of his trailer, his very sore chin tucked deep into his jacket. A fat robin yanked a worm up out of the ground and flew away as he rounded the corner of the bunkhouse, his shoulders hunched against the nip in the morning air. Clouds hung low, but the sun broke through on the far side of the pasture where Skye's cattle grazed. He shook the ladder that was leaning against the granary. Water splashed down on his hat. Slippery, no doubt, and since he hadn't felt like sacrificing his chin again, he wore running shoes to work in today. Hopefully the soles would give him better traction. As it was, he was going to get soaked climbing around on the wet roof, but so be it. More afternoon showers were forecast for that day, and he wanted to get as much done as possible.

He heard the door to Skye's house slam and the sound of her boots on the porch. The odds were that he would have help today, since it was Skye's day off. The woman was bound and determined to maintain as much control of her place as possible, and he was good with that—as long as she didn't put herself in jeopardy...like, say, by climbing a slippery ladder onto a slippery roof. She'd probably say he was being sexist, but it was more like being protective…of a woman who didn't want to be protected.

Skye crossed the gravel driveway, hands pushed deep into her sweatshirt pockets. She had on faded blue jeans and a canvas vest over her hoodie. Her hair was spilling out from under the hood she had pulled up over her head. As she got closer, she raised her gaze from the gravel to meet his, her expression cool, almost serene, as if she knew exactly what lay ahead that day and how she was going to handle it.

He, on the other hand, didn't have a clue. Would they talk? Not talk? Get into yet another argument about roofs and ladders? Would he notice her perfume and her hair and wish that things were different between them, just as he had in her kitchen last night? She probably wouldn't be thrilled to know he thought things like that.

"Morning," she said in a low voice. "How's your chin?"

"Sore as hell."

"As it should be." She stopped a few feet away from him, and he sensed the huge chasm separating them. Because of Mason? Because he was who he was? Because she was used to seeing him as the enemy?

Last night he'd felt a shift between them, then Skye had done a mental one-eighty, as if she couldn't handle the idea of being attracted to a guy like him.

"Do you like the way things are between us, Skye?"

A startled look crossed her face. "I don't—"

"I think you do," he interrupted. "I'm not your enemy, Skye."

"Of course you're not my enemy." She jammed her

hands back into her pockets and pursed her lips in a way that told Tyler that there were a lot of things she wanted to say, but that she was afraid of revealing too much. So he shifted his weight and waited. Sometimes stubbornness was a good quality. "We are not enemies," she said carefully. "But we aren't actually friends either."

"And why is that?"

"Friends feel easy around one another. I feel easy around Jess."

"You don't feel easy around me?" He knew she didn't, had seen more than enough evidence last night in her kitchen to confirm the fact—but he asked the question anyway. Maybe it was a jerk thing to do, but he wanted to hear her answer. Wanted to know where he was lacking.

She lifted her chin and met his challenge with the truth. "I feel edgy around you, Tyler."

"Yeah. I've kind of sensed that," he said drily. "My question is why do you feel that way?"

If her hands went any deeper into the pockets, they would come out the other side. "You're different from Jess."

"I'm the bad twin, you mean?"

"If that's the way you want to put it." She casually backed up a step or two, then stopped and shifted her weight to one side, hands still in her pockets. "Jess was friendly and supportive and never once did anything to make me feel self-conscious."

"Back to that, are we?"

"You've got to understand, Tyler… I spent a lot of years thinking of you as the…" Her mouth flattened. "I'm *not* going to say enemy."

"What synonym will you choose?" he asked grimly.

"Nemesis. You threatened me with reptiles, for pity's sake."

He took a step closer. "But I think we both know that it isn't the reptiles that we're dealing with now."

She let out a self-conscious sigh. "I made you out as the bad guy with Mason, and...well...I believed it. But I apologized."

"Do you still believe that I was the bad guy?" He needed to know.

"I...don't know. I no longer think you encouraged him to gamble."

"But..."

"You're two of a kind. I think you encouraged him to be wild."

"I did. Although he didn't need encouragement, Skye."

She took another step back, even though she was already a good distance away from him, and pulled her hands out of her back pockets, folding them over her chest. "I've lost my husband, I almost lost my ranch. I've been through hell this past year. I don't need to hear this."

"It's the truth, Skye. I liked Mason, but I accepted the truth about him."

"Because it didn't affect you." She moistened her lips then abruptly announced, "I hate feeling uncomfortable on my own ranch."

And there it was. He made her uncomfortable by just...being there.

"I guess you'll have to go back to the bank."

She swallowed. "You know I can't do that."

"Then I suppose you want me to move off the ranch?"

It was obvious she wanted to say yes, and he had no idea why she didn't, for no other reason than to show him how she felt about him. But instead she said, "We need a…treaty…or something. Rules. That's it. We need rules."

"Okay. Make some rules."

A pained expression crossed her face. "Why is everything so impossible with you?"

"Something to do with my winning personality, I guess."

She didn't answer immediately but instead studied his face closely, as if trying to find the answer to some mystery there. Even without the stitches, he wasn't pretty at the moment. He knew that. Not unless she was a woman who liked yellowish-brown circles around eyes and remnant suture marks above the bridge of the nose. But her gaze did not linger on his injuries. It traveled down to his mouth and held, and he felt his body stir in response.

"Skye?" Her gaze jerked up to his as if he'd just startled her out of a daydream. "Make some damned rules so that we can go work on the roof."

She gave her head a slow shake. "What good would it do? Bull riders are born to break rules."

"Except for Jess?"

"I have a feeling he's no angel either."

Tyler couldn't help it. He smiled. "I'd like to make a rule."

She shot him a startled look. "Which is?"

"We talk about everyday stuff. The kind of stuff

you would talk to Jess about. I look like him. It seems to me that you could pretend."

"You don't look like him," she said as she knelt to open the toolbox and take out a hammer.

"You mean the black eyes?"

She stopped with her hand on top of the box. "No. I mean you don't look like him."

"We're identical twins."

She shook her head and started toward the building with the ladder leaning against it. Tyler stood frozen, then started after her. He really wanted more of an explanation, but he'd just made a rule, and it seemed important not to break it—especially when she expected him to do just that.

THE SUN PEEKED out from behind a cloud as Tyler went to get the tractor. After a brief consultation, they'd decided to use the bucket to lift the bundles of shingles to the roof, thereby avoiding numerous trips up and down the still-damp ladder, and also avoiding any future ladder accidents.

As she waited, Skye climbed up to the roof and looked out over the ranch that she loved…loved and sacrificed for. It was a sacrifice having Tyler here, especially when she was becoming so aware of him in ways she hadn't expected, but she needed to stop taking it out on him. Therefore, she was going to do exactly as he'd suggested—talk about neutral stuff.

Pretend he was Jess. She didn't know how successful she would be, because he wasn't Jess. He was darker, more unpredictable. More attractive. But…she had to do something to create a more peaceful environment on her ranch. An environment that didn't have her feeling jumpy and defensive.

The tractor fired to life, and after allowing it to warm up for a few minutes, Tyler brought it out of the shed and headed toward the granary. He stopped and set down the bucket, then climbed down from the driver's seat and started pulling the bundles of shingles into the bucket before Skye reached the ground. She put a hand on his shoulder to get his attention, since the engine noise was loud, and his gaze jerked toward her, as if he was startled that *she* had touched *him* instead of the other way around.

"Let me," she said. She took hold of the shingles and pulled, groaning a little as she realized just how heavy a whole bundle was. When Tyler leaned down to help, she waved him off. "I can do it."

And she did. It took a little time, but at least Tyler wasn't ripping his shoulder up. She let out a breath and stood, dusting her hands off on her pants. "If you rip your shoulder again, you'll be here for six weeks instead of four."

"And we wouldn't want that, would we?"

"Just thinking about you and your career."

"Bull."

Skye straightened up and looked him square in the face. "I thought we were aiming for neutral. And, for the record, I was being truthful. I know how difficult it is for you guys to be off the circuit."

There'd been a big learning curve after she'd married Mason, but she'd eventually come to understand that her guy needed to ride the way some people needed to climb mountains. It was something deeply ingrained in his psyche, and she'd come to a place where she could support his needs. Understand them. And it worked. She went to events when they were close by, but mostly she stayed at home and kept the ranch running. Mason made it home more often than a lot of his buddies.

Tyler gave a curt nod and headed back to the tractor and revved the engine.

"Ready?" he asked over the noise.

"Yes," she called back and then started climbing. He waited until she was safely on the roof before lifting the bucket with the shingles and the tools. Fifteen minutes later, the bundles were deposited on either side of the roof and Tyler had demonstrated the not very complex task of laying shingles and hammering them into place. And since Skye refused to relinquish the hammer, Tyler flopped the shingles into place and she nailed them down. They continued their assembly-line work until Tyler called for a break about an hour in. They sat a couple of feet apart on the small roof and looked out over the ranch, just as Skye had done earlier.

"Your chicken house is coming along nicely," Tyler said as he gestured toward the single frame lying where she'd started working on it behind the barn.

"Funny," she muttered, but she took no offense. This was a good neutral topic—the first they'd hit upon. Until the break, they'd worked in silence.

"It's not very big. More like a chicken apartment."

"I only want four or five hens. Enough to keep me in eggs and to eat the bugs. I had a few hens when I was a kid and they roosted in the barn, but the raccoons and owls played hell with them. I promised myself that if I got chickens, they would have a safe place to sleep."

"Your goose sleeps in the barn unmolested."

"Vanessa is a tough old girl."

"I noticed."

She was about to ask what he meant when he pointed into the distance. "Are those our pastures there?"

"Yes. But the ones beyond…those belong to Cliff."

"Ah. We need to ride the boundary sometime soon. Check fences."

"I'll have to borrow a horse from my neighbor Lex." Lex—Alexa—was married to one of Mason's friends, and because of that had become her friend.

"There are two horses in the pasture," Tyler pointed out.

"Buzz is chronically lame."

"You're feeding a lame horse?"

She looked out over the pasture where Buzz and her other very ridable horse, Pepper, were eating. Buzz had a solid pedigree and had cost Mason a lot of money, but a bone spur had put an end to his usefulness. Skye loved him, just as she'd loved Mr. Joe. It made her feel good having him around, and at this point in her life, she was all about anything that gave her peace and good feelings.

Skye pushed her hair back again, a nervous gesture that was becoming a tell. "The alternative to feeding a lame horse is to put him down. The vet assures me he's in no real pain as long as he doesn't bear weight, and I'm not going to kill him."

The stark words hung for a moment, practically echoing between them. But Skye meant them with all of her heart. There'd been enough death associated with her ranch of late.

"I wasn't judging you," Tyler said in an uncharacteristically soft voice, making her feel embarrassed for her own quick judgment.

"I'm sorry," she said. "It's…"

"A habit?"

She gave a nod. "A bad one, apparently." Tyler shifted his gaze to stare out over the distance, while Skye sucked in an audible breath. "Look. I'm sorry."

He turned his head to look at her. "Me, too."

"Why?"

"I forced my way onto your ranch."

Her mouth flattened grimly. "Thus allowing me to keep it."

A gust of wind swept over them, and Tyler reached for the shingles. "We'd better get back to work."

Deep blue-gray clouds were building in the distance, and even though, for reasons she couldn't fathom, Skye wanted to continue the conversation, settle things once and for all, she gave a nod of agreement and took up her hammer.

They managed to lay most of the roof before the rain started, and then there was no question of continuing as the skies opened and rain began hammering on the roof, fat drops bouncing and splashing around them. They scrambled for the ladder, Tyler going first, and then waiting at the bottom for Skye. His big hands settled on her waist as her foot slipped and stayed there until she was safely on the ground. Without a word, they dashed to the nearby safety of the barn.

"The nail can is still on the roof," Skye said after they had raced through the wide-open double doors.

"I'm not going after it," Tyler said in a serious voice.

In spite of herself, Skye smiled. Their gazes connected and Tyler smiled back, and suddenly there were butterflies beating inside Skye's chest. She'd never realized what a devastating smile Tyler Hayward had. And if she'd wanted to double-check her findings, she would have been out of luck, because it faded instantly and his usual cocky half smile took its place.

Self-protection?

The thought came out of nowhere.

"If you want, I can do the chores on the days you work afternoons."

"Yeah. About that…" Her hands went deeper into her pockets, stretching the heavy gray knit fabric. "You don't need to feed."

"It's not a problem."

"I like to do it. It's part of my unwinding."

Tyler smiled again, but it wasn't the same smile as before. It was…guarded. "Feeding that mean-ass goose is part of your unwinding?"

"What did Vanessa do to you?" Because it was obvious from his tone that she'd done something.

"Scared the crap out of me. I let myself into the barn, and she came at me flapping wings and hissing. She got me up onto the hay."

Skye laughed. "I can't say I wouldn't have loved to have seen that."

"Maybe she'll do it again." He jerked his head toward the wide doors at the far end of the barn where Vanessa was strutting back and forth as she watched the rain.

"She's not a big fan of strangers. She wasn't even that fond of Mason."

"But she likes you."

"I raised her. I found her as a baby at the creek. Something must have happened to the mother. I brought her home and put her under a heat lamp, and as you can see, she thrived. Mason was pretty surprised to find a little goose in our bedroom when he came home."

"You let her roam?"

"She was in a box. A really big box that took up most of the bedroom floor. I didn't want her to feel lonely. Also, I could monitor Jinx, my cat, until he came to realize that she was part of our family." Her expression brightened. "I have the cutest picture of the two of them curled up together in the yard." And then she seemed to remember that he was Tyler and not Jess.

"Maybe you could show me sometime."

"Yes," she said. "Maybe."

Translation: probably not.

"How much do you feed Goosezilla?"

She let out a small snort and shook her head, but didn't look at him. "A scoop of mash and some grain scattered on the ground. She likes to forage. If I have vegetable scraps, I bring them to her. Maybe you could give her some of your veggie scraps after one of your precisely portioned muscle-building meals and make friends." She smiled a little. "And then maybe she won't put you up on the hay."

"I will consider it."

She moved onto the haystack just inside the door, expertly rolled a bale down and pulled a jackknife out of her pocket to cut the strings. "So tell me more about this diet of yours." Safe topic.

"It's not a diet in the weight-loss sense. It's a diet in a nutritional sense. I have to do what I can to maintain muscle, so I don't waste calories on empty carbs."

"Do you do yoga?"

"Tried. Not my thing. I have some stretches and some balances." He gave her a quick look. "What kind of program did Mason follow at home?"

"He ate pretty normal, but liked steak that we could afford sometimes and not others. He did yoga." She gave him a curious look. "If you don't do yoga, what kind of balancing do you do?"

"I stand on a ball, try not to fall off."

"Interesting."

"Kind of funny to watch. You should have seen me when I started. Even with a medicine ball, I ended up on my butt a couple times."

"Yes, it's always good to have a program in which you can get hurt while practicing."

He gave her a crooked smile. "That's kind of what my profession is all about."

Chapter Ten

When it became obvious that the rain was not going to let up, Skye and Tyler went to their separate abodes to spend their evenings alone. Skye told herself she was good with this, but the truth was that after having a rather decent conversation with Tyler in the barn, her house seemed lonelier than usual. Which was crazy. Why would she be hungry for human contact when she worked in a very people-centered occupation?

It made no sense. And neither did pulling back the curtain before she went to bed to see if it was still raining and Tyler's lights were still on. The answers to those questions were no and yes. She had to work the morning shift the next day but fully intended to get back up on the roof when she got home. The quicker they got the roof done, the better.

She also thought about crossing the distance to Tyler's door and asking him not to get on the roof when she wasn't there.

She didn't.

He wouldn't agree, and she wasn't going to put herself in a position of arguing with him. Things were so much less stressful when they didn't argue. Could they possibly continue in this mode? Because it would probably be years before she could make a serious dent in what she owed him, so it really made sense to broker peace between them.

Yes. Peace.

And maybe that would help her deal with the edgy feeling she had whenever he got close to her.

Skye got off shift a little early the next day and arrived home to find that Tyler had finished one roof and had a start on the next. She changed her clothes, retrieved her hammer out of the toolbox and climbed up to join him on the roof.

"How was work?" he asked, as if having her show up to roof was a normal part of his day.

"Not very busy. I like it better when I'm busy." She reached into the nail can, grabbed a handful, then gestured for him to lay the next shingle. He did, and she nailed it into place.

They moved to their left. Tyler laid another shingle, and Skye hammered it in. "You know that I can hammer, right? That I hammered for a couple of hours before you got here?"

"Guess that makes it my turn." She hit a nail in with one satisfying blow. "You shouldn't be doing this at all while you're healing, but I know better than to argue with you."

"Know me that well?"

She leveled a look at him. "I know your species." She hit a nail wrong and sent it sailing off the roof, then put another in place and tried again. "When Mason and I married, I thought I understood bull riders, but I still had a few things to learn. Now I get it."

"And you were good with all the time he spent on the road?"

"I missed him." She couldn't say she was good with all the time she'd spent alone, but she understood it. Figured it was temporary. A guy's body could take the stress of bull riding for only so long. Once Mason retired, they'd have a ton of time together, working the ranch...that had been the plan anyway.

Skye let out a sigh. Plans. Yeah. She hit another nail.

Tyler flopped another shingle in place, and she moved toward him to hammer. They made a good team, covered some decent ground, but they would have done better had they been on separate roofs. She meant what she said about him not stressing his shoulder for at least one more day. Even hammering with his off hand had to jar his healing muscles.

"I hope I'm not treading into the land of things I don't want to know, but were you and Paige once close?" There. She'd said it as if she didn't care—and, of course, she shouldn't care. Paige was an impressive woman, and Tyler could do a lot worse. However, when Paige had questioned her that day about Tyler's role on the ranch, she'd rather resented it...and once again suspected that Paige had a thing for her ranching partner.

"We kind of started the journey, but it didn't go very far."

Ka-ching. "Ah. Well, I think she's interested in starting again."

"Huh."

Skye couldn't tell if that was a good *huh* or a bad *huh*. It was a purposely neutral *huh*, and perhaps that was a sign that she needed to keep to neutral topics, even if she wanted a more definitive answer. "What will you do when you retire?"

Tyler was silent for a moment. "You mean if I'm

not working the ranch here with you and bringing in huge profits?"

Skye laughed. Huge profits and ranching rarely went hand in hand. People ranched because they loved the land and the life. When she glanced over at Tyler, his cheeks were creased in a most pleasant way, and when he slowly turned his head to meet her gaze, amusement lit his eyes—eyes that were even more attractive without the stitches between them.

Something stirred low in Skye's abdomen as their gazes connected, but she did her best to ignore the sensation as she said, "Yes. Exactly. Let's say the unimaginable happens and the ranch is barely making enough to sustain us both…or I manage to pay off the paper and we dissolve the partnership. What are you going to do then?"

"Tough question, Skye."

Even though the nails were short, she managed to pound the next one in crooked. She was about to hit it hard and bury the bent head when Tyler held his hand out for the hammer. Without a word, she handed it to him and he pulled the nail, then handed it back. "We could have flattened it, but I like all my nails straight."

Skye gave him a curious look. "I'd never peg you as a straight-nail kind of guy."

"There is a lot about me you don't know, sweet…" His mouth tightened as the words trailed off. "…person."

Skye fought another smile, which was happening more frequently than she would have thought possible. "Sweet person?"

"Beats sweet cheeks." He shot her a look. "You need to tell me who that guy is."

"Not a chance." Todd Lundgren, local golden boy ex-football star, wouldn't stand a chance against Tyler.

"Back to what I'm going to do... I want to raise some cattle."

"Bucking stock?"

"No. I'll leave that to Hennessey. He seems to have gotten a good start. The young ones look good. I'll never ride one, but Cody might."

"Cattle won't support you—unless you own land outright...or you're still here."

"And you assume I won't be."

"Not when you're say...fifty."

He cast her a sidelong look. "You're saying you don't want to grow old with me?"

Skye sputtered and focused on hammering so she didn't nail crookedly again. That didn't require an answer. It also didn't require her insides doing a free fall. What was it about this guy? The forbidden-fruit aspect maybe?

"My plan," he continued on a serious note, "is to bank the money you pay me back. I get interest on the paper and I get interest from the bank. As long as no one I know gets too seriously banged up, I'll save the money and buy a new place where I will be able to be supported by raising and selling cattle." He flopped down a shingle. "That is my plan."

The part about no one getting seriously injured got her attention. Bull riders did tend to help one another. She and Mason had donated to medical funds when they'd been able. "You need to think about your own future, too." She reached in the can for another few nails. "But I know it's a thin line to walk."

"It could be me. I mean I have some bare-bones insurance, but it costs."

The sun came out from behind the clouds, and while it felt good at first, it wasn't long until it was beating down on them and both Tyler and Skye were shedding coats, vests and sweatshirts. Finally, she told Tyler that she needed a break to grab something to eat.

"Meet back here in fifteen minutes?" he asked as he wiped the back of his sleeve over his forehead and then put his ball cap back into place.

"Don't eat any Twinkies." She turned and headed back to the house, whistling under her breath. She, on the other hand, was totally going to eat a Twinkie. She loved them.

As TYLER WATCHED Skye walk away, he wondered if she was aware of just how far her barriers had dropped that day. Neutral topics. Who would have thought it?

He felt as if he might have moved a few steps closer to convincing Skye that, beneath the bad-twin facade, he was just as good of a guy as Jess was. As good as her late husband, if not better, because at least he was honest.

Tyler shook off the thought. The past was the past.

When Tyler got to his trailer, he reached into his small fridge and pulled out the almond butter, opened it and dipped a spoon in, eating it straight out of the jar. Twinkie indeed. Although, truthfully? He'd eat a carton of them if they were available. That was why he didn't have cookies or sweets in his house. There'd be time to indulge later, when he wasn't so dependent on his body being the best it could be. When what his brother called "real life" started.

As if he wasn't living real life now.

The last roof was almost done. Skye worked again tomorrow, and he intended to have it finished by the time she got home. He rolled his shoulder, knew that while he might not be doing it damage, he wasn't helping the healing process any. But it was his fault that the buildings had no roofs, and he was going to make certain they were fixed before he left. When they were done roofing, he'd ride the property, check the fences... and for that he needed a horse. Or maybe a mule.

He dipped into the jar again. He'd have to ask Skye what the mule's infirmity was, because all her animals seemed to have one. She had a lame horse, a chronically mean goose, an escape-artist donkey and an oversize cat, who was the most normal member of her menagerie. As far as he knew anyway.

He and Skye had barely made it back outside before another storm started blowing in and he suggested that they call it a day. Surprisingly she agreed, so Tyler got into his truck and headed off to Hennessey's to watch the riders and shoot the breeze with his own kind.

When he arrived, he was surprised to see Angie Salinas standing close to Cody. The last he'd heard she'd been dating his cousin Blaine, but since neither Blaine nor Angie had a reputation for sticking with one person for too long, maybe it wasn't that much of a surprise to see her with Cody. "Hey, Angie."

"Tyler." Angie cocked her head at him. "Aren't you supposed to be putting a roof on a building?"

"We're done for the day," he said, coming to lean on the fence next to her.

Cody stepped closer as if Tyler were encroaching. *Fear not, kid.* Angie was a likable girl, but not his type.

"You're roofing?" Cody asked.

Angie shot Cody a look. "Tyler got scammed by a roofing company," she explained matter-of-factly. There were no secrets in this town—at least not between the women who worked at the café.

"Honestly?"

Tyler shrugged philosophically. "They took my money, started the job, then closed doors."

"Sucks."

"Yeah. It does."

Angie reached out to touch Tyler's arm, bringing his attention back to her. "Is Skye really helping you? On the roof, I mean?"

"Yep. Building a chicken house, too. She's good with a hammer."

"No kidding." Angie looked as if she didn't know whether or not to believe him. He decided to let her work it out for herself.

Tyler nodded at Cody and moved to the far side of the arena, where Jasper Hennessey and his brother, Bill, were talking to a couple of high school kids. They asked Tyler his opinion on the mandatory use of helmets, which he fully supported. After this last ride, he was going to become a helmet wearer, himself.

Angie continued her flirt-fest with Cody, so Tyler ambled over to where Trace Delaney and Grady Owen were standing near a gate, deep in conversation. He slowed his steps as he approached, not wanting to interrupt, but Grady waved him over.

"It looked like you guys were discussing important matters."

"Actually, we were discussing logistics," Grady said. "Annie wants to travel with Trace for a week, so Lex is going to watch the twins instead of coming with me. It's a matter of who stays where."

"Life seems to get complicated when you marry," Tyler said. It wasn't that long ago that both Trace and Grady were single and their only worry was staying healthy and getting to the next event.

Trace nodded. "Throw in twins and, yeah, it can get…interesting." But he smiled in a way which clearly indicated that he liked his new role as a husband and father. Tyler had to admit that Annie Owen was a sweetheart and her eight-year-old twin girls always made him smile.

"Even without twins, it gets interesting," Grady said.

Tyler snorted. "Yeah, but you married Lex."

Grady grinned. "Point taken." He pulled his phone out of his pocket and glanced at the time. "Speaking of which, I need to get going. We're painting the upstairs bedrooms, and I promised I'd be back in time for paint consultation."

"Yeah," Trace agreed. "Annie and I are taking the girls shopping for winter coats as soon as I get back. I'm better at coats than dresses."

"Not me," Grady said. "I'm a party dress shopping fool."

The guys laughed and Tyler smiled, feeling as if he'd just wandered into a new, strange land where he wasn't familiar with the customs and mores.

"Are things going okay on the ranch?" Trace asked.

"As well as can be expected. As you can imagine, Skye and I are working out a few things, but…you know. It's always that way when you start something new."

Trace and Grady exchanged a quick look, telling

Tyler that his arrangement with Skye had most probably been a topic of discussion in the Delaney-Owen households. He expected no less. Bull riders kept track of their own.

"Let us know if you need any help around the place," Grady offered.

"We have it covered for now, but thanks." He emphasized the word *we*, as if he needed to let these family men know that he wasn't alone in the world. He had a twin on the other side of Montana and a business partner who wanted him anywhere but on her ranch.

After Trace and Grady left, Tyler drifted back to the rails and watched a few more rides, then said his good-byes and headed to his home that wasn't really a home.

Meanwhile, Trace and Grady were going home to women who wanted to see them.

What would it be like?

"I HAVE TO admit that I didn't believe you when you said you were helping with the roof," Angie admitted as she loaded glasses onto a tray. It was her last day of work before she left for cosmetology school in Missoula for the next six months, and she was moving with tortoise-like speed—not that Skye blamed her. Angie had wanted to get out of the café forever, and Tiffani Crenshaw had already offered her a position in her salon when she'd finished her course of study, which meant that the gossip capacity of the beauty shop would be doubled by next spring.

Skye gave a small snort. "Why would I lie about helping with the roof?"

Angie tossed her head. "To mess with me?"

There had been occasions when people had told

Angie a false story just to watch it spread. It was a lot like putting a dye marker in a lake.

"If I decide to mess with you, it'd be with a better story than that."

"Is roofing hard work?"

"Easy to do, but tedious and time-consuming." Especially when they kept having to break for weather. But if all went well, they would be done that afternoon.

"I'd spend a day on the roof with Tyler Hayward," Angie volunteered, still slowly transferring the glassware. "But Cody's pretty cute, don't you think?"

"Very." It was hard not to be with a bull rider's build, green eyes and longish blond hair. "Just…be aware of what you're getting into if you date a bull rider."

Angie set down the tray. "What?"

Skye held up a finger, indicating that Angie should hold her thought, before heading around her tables, checking on her customers. When she got back, she said, "It's hard to explain until you experience it, but a serious bull rider can't help himself. He lives for the ride. Most other things take second place."

"Like girlfriends?"

Skye didn't know how to answer that, because it depended on the bull rider and the relationship.

"Their careers are generally fairly short," she offered as a positive.

"And if they aren't?"

"Be prepared to pray and worry and leave things to a higher power for eight seconds several times a week during the season." Skye leaned her hip against the counter. "What I'm trying to say is that these guys are focused. If you can't live with their career, then don't date a bull rider."

"Thanks for the warning...I think."

"It's something you need to know." Skye reached out and touched Angie's arm. "Forewarned is forearmed and all that."

Angie blew out a breath. "Guess I'll find out what I'm capable of."

"Guess so. And, yes, Cody is adorable."

Angie smiled. "I know! And guess what he told me about Trace and Annie? They're thinking of trying for a baby."

"How does he...?" Skye shook her head as she held up a hand. "Never mind. I don't want to know. And maybe Trace and Annie want this kept quiet?"

Angie looked surprised at the concept. "Huh. Maybe."

The door opened, and a group of six teens headed for the booth in the back. "Better start the fries," Skye called back to the kitchen. "The after-school crowd is here."

Angie sauntered over to the table as Skye wiped the counter again. Angie was twenty-five and meant no harm...but her mouth was practically a lethal weapon at times. It'd certainly gotten Skye in trouble when Angie had mentioned that Skye thought Tyler was trying to buy a clear conscience by investing in the ranch. There was no way she wanted the same thing to happen to Annie Owen.

BABE'S HEAD WAS hanging over the fence, his long ears tipped forward, when Skye parked her car close to the house. As soon as she opened the car door, he gave a long, plaintive call. Chester was on the move again.

She grabbed her tote bag and crossed the driveway to the mule, stroking the side of his face as she told him that she'd find his little friend and bring him back as soon as she changed her clothes. Babe was not mollified by her response, and as soon as she turned to go to the house he let out another loud, creaky call for his little buddy.

Skye changed into jeans and flannel shirt, shoved her feet into running shoes and barely took time to tie them. Stepping out onto the porch, she stood for a moment surveying the immediate vicinity, looking for a furry gray bundle of trouble. Nothing. Tyler's truck was not in its usual spot, and all the roofs were completely finished. Maybe he was out looking for Chester, or maybe he'd left before the little guy had escaped. One thing she was certain of—now that the roofing disaster was over, they were going to work on securing the fence so that the donkey stayed put.

Skye trotted down the porch steps and started looking in all the usual donkey-hiding places—the barn where the hay was stored, the compost pile out back, the garden. No sign of a mini-donkey. Skye stood in the driveway with her hands on her hips. He'd never left the property, and she was certain he wouldn't leave it now, unless he'd been chased off. He had no fear of coyotes, but maybe a larger animal had passed through…

Her stomach was starting to knot, and for the first time since he'd arrived, Skye wished that Tyler was there. She could use the help scouring the property.

She started toward the large pasture, thinking he might be on the other side in the trees, then abruptly shifted course.

The orchard.

The apples were down due to the wind and frost, and

there was nothing Chester liked more than old apples. However, he'd never before gotten through the fence to help himself to any. Today, however, proved different… not only had he finagled his way through the fence, he was lying on his side at the edge of the orchard.

Skye started running when she saw the small gray heap lying just inside the fence. Her thoughts jumbled as she dashed the last few yards—he'd eaten too many apples, colicked, rolled, twisted his gut…her beloved donkey was dead or dying. Only he wasn't dead. Skye could hear his raspy, labored breath as she skidded to a stop at his side. If he was colicked, she needed to get him to his feet.

Within seconds she realized he wasn't colicked. Instead he was wrapped—tightly wrapped—in old barbed wire that was cutting into the skin of his neck and legs. Skye tried to loosen the wire, find the end. It was too tight, too tangled.

The sound of a motor brought her head up, and she jumped to her feet. Chester struggled, and she instantly sank back down next to him, stroking his neck and telling him it would be okay.

"I have to get tools," she murmured, hoping the little animal would understand her tone of voice. Rising to her feet, she started across the pasture toward the house. Tyler was on the way to his trailer when she shouted his name. She shouted again, and he stopped, then turned. As soon as he saw her, he started toward her with long, purposeful strides. She broke into a jog, and they met at the fence.

"What's wrong?" He was already climbing through the rails.

"We need nippers. Chester is rolled up in wire." She pointed to where she'd left him. "In the old orchard."

"I'll get the tools."

Tyler climbed back through the fence, and Skye started back toward where the donkey lay. The poor little guy was ripped and cut, and she needed to get him free. Tyler must have had his tools at the ready, because she'd barely reached Chester's side when she heard him running through the grass toward them. A few seconds later he was beside her. He knelt and began testing the wire wrapped around the little donkey's legs and neck. Chester took a painful breath, and Skye ran her hand over his wiry coat.

"Here, I think." Tyler struggled to get the nippers in between the wire and skin, then snipped. The wire loosened an iota, allowing him better access to the next strand. Skye continued to pet Chester, murmuring words of encouragement as Tyler moved around the little donkey, snipping wire and tossing pieces aside. When he got the last bit free, he sank down next to Skye and ran his big hand over the donkey.

"He has thick skin. Amazing that he's not cut up more than he is."

Indeed, a horse in the same circumstances would have had larger, more gaping wounds. "Small blessings," Skye murmured. "We need to get him up. If we can't, then I guess we'll get the tractor."

They didn't need the tractor. After a few more seconds lying on his side, Chester seemed to understand that he was totally free and lifted his head. With help from Tyler and Skye, he got to his feet, then stood, shaking, his head hanging down.

"Maybe I should try to carry him."

"He weighs more than two hundred pounds."

Before Tyler could argue the point, or sacrifice his shoulder, Chester took a shaky step forward and then another. With Skye on one side and Tyler on the other, they maneuvered the donkey back to the ranch proper. Skye opened the man gate, and Tyler urged the little guy through. After that he headed straight for his distraught mule buddy. Tyler nudged him toward the barn, and Babe trotted into his stall to keep an eye on his friend while Tyler and Skye doctored him.

Together they cleaned the cuts, gave the donkey a tetanus shot and big dose of penicillin, then turned him loose in a small pen in the barn where he was knee-deep in clean straw. Babe crowded as close to the dividing fence as he could get, nudging his buddy with his nose.

"I thought I'd lost him," Skye said. "When I found him lying still under that tree…I thought he'd colicked and died." She felt the sting of tears and swallowed hard. Reaction, pure and simple, but she wasn't giving in. The donkey was alive. She'd been terrified of losing yet another thing in her life, but hey—hadn't happened. A tear rolled down her face anyway, and Skye swiped at it with her sleeve.

"Are you okay?" Tyler asked.

"Fine. All's well…" Her voice thickened, and she let the words hang. Then, in a move that seemed ridiculously right, Tyler put an arm around her without taking his eyes off the donkey, who was thinking about bedding down, and pulled her close to his side. Skye didn't fight him. Not even a little. She leaned into his comforting warmth, closed her eyes, drew in his scent. Felt the need stir inside her.

Step away.

She did not. She was tired of fighting, tired of worrying. Tired of everything being a battle. Tyler didn't move, but his grip had tightened on her shoulder as she relaxed against him. He smelled good, he felt safe—which only proved how stressed and tired she was. And when he did move—when he looked down at her and then lifted her chin with his thumb and forefinger—she did not allow herself to think. Thinking would ruin everything.

Her eyes drifted closed again, and a second later his lips lightly touched hers, just as she'd known they would. She let out a soft breath, felt it move across his skin. Tyler hesitated, as if he were afraid of doing too much, too soon. A wise man, Tyler, because this was too much, too soon. Skye did not care. Her lips parted against his as she slid a hand up around his neck, felt the hair beneath her palm, the solidness of his chest beneath her other hand. The kiss deepened, and Skye lost herself. She hadn't kissed a man other than her husband in years and years, had forgotten the rush, the taste, the excitement…

She eased back, her lips lingering on his for another long second before she broke contact. Tyler dropped his arm, allowing his hand to slide down to hers before falling away. Skye drew in a breath and decided that the very last thing in the world she wanted to do was to address what had just happened. So instead she gave him a weary half smile.

"Strange day."

He hesitated, then smiled back at her. "That's one way to put it."

"I should get back to the house." For no reason other

than the need to escape while she could. "I'm on shift tomorrow, but when I get off, can we talk about beefing up donkey security?"

"You bet. I don't want this to happen again."

"Yeah." Chester was going to hate total confinement, but he was going to have to give up his Houdini ways for his own health and welfare—as well as Skye's. She couldn't take many more afternoons like the one she'd just had.

Chapter Eleven

Mason's ashes had been scattered on the mountains behind the ranch, so on the occasion of his birthday, two days after Chester's traumatic wire incident, Skye had no memorial to visit. Instead she walked into the pasture and stood for a long time staring at the gorgeous mountain range that was her husband's final resting place.

Last year, when she'd stood in this spot, she'd been raw with pain from her loss. This year...she felt differently. She missed him. But she was also angry at him for leaving her in the circumstances she was now in.

I supported you and you betrayed me.

He'd had a disease. Gambling addiction was like alcoholism. Mason hadn't been able to help himself because he hadn't yet admitted he had a problem. Skye believed in her heart that he would have...but she didn't know what it would have taken for him to make that admission. He'd drained their bank account and hadn't told her anything.

He thought he'd win the money back.

He was young and wild and with time would have settled.

Maybe.

Looking at the man his father had been, there was always the possibility that he would have maintained his wild ways. His father was a good man, funny and caring, despite the fact that he was less than dependable when push came to shove. He meant well…and he was married to a woman who managed his life for him.

Mason had been similar to his father in temperament, as she was very similar to Mason's mother. No relationship was perfect, and for the most part they had done well together, her and Mason. She loved him. She missed him. And she regretted that she never got the chance to discover what Mason might have been capable of after his bull-riding career was over. He was good on the ranch, when he had the time to do the work, finish his projects. He partied hard, he worked hard. He rode hard.

He'd lied to her and left her with nothing.

The conflict between anger and love was killing her. Would next year be any better? Would she have a firmer grip on things? Understand more than she did now…be able to fully and totally forgive?

And damn it, would Tyler still be on the ranch, tempting her and taunting her?

She left the pasture, because it seemed wrong to have thoughts of another man crowd her on the day she was contemplating her husband's day of birth, and walked to the grave of Mr. Joe.

Another loss. Devastating, but expected. Losing Mason—devastating beyond words. The discoveries that followed…also devastating. And then came Tyler—unexpected white knight. He'd had a crush on her way back when, and judging what had happened between them two days before, he still had feelings for her. Or felt sorry for her. Poor Skye. Another near-loss.

Her jaw muscles tightened at the thought of being an object of pity.

But this crazy feeling dancing around inside her wasn't one-sided and was not the result of pity—she was certain of that. She was also dead certain that this crazy feeling was dangerous. Beyond dangerous, because it could blow her peaceful existence to smithereens. Tyler was attractive—in a way his twin was not—and if she could do it with an iron-clad guarantee of no consequences now or ever, she wouldn't mind getting closer to him, playing with fire.

But consequences and bad circumstances had been coming at her over the past couple of years, and she was not going to tempt fate. Nope.

She and Tyler were business partners and nothing more, and she needed to make certain that he understood that…and she needed to make certain her errant hormones were aware.

The rain increased in intensity, running down her vinyl coat, soaking into her jeans, clinging to the ends of her eyelashes, but she couldn't bring herself to move. Tyler was almost to her when she finally heard his footsteps in the wet grass over the sound of the rain and turned to see him sloshing across the pasture.

He stopped a few feet in front of her. "Is something wrong?"

Nothing. Everything.

"It's Mason's birthday."

There was a slight shift in his expression, but he said nothing as he reached out to take her arm and start her moving toward the house. His hand slid down over the sleeve of her damp coat, and his warm fingers laced with hers. "Do you get some great joy out of getting soaked to the skin?"

"The rain makes me aware."

"Of what?" he asked without slowing his steps.

"Being alive." She felt his grip tighten on her fingers before it loosened again.

They ducked under the porch cover, and as soon as they were out of the weather, Tyler let go of her hand and brushed the water off his lower face. "I was worried about you. I didn't know it was Mason's birthday."

"I felt like I had to acknowledge," she murmured. "He was my husband."

"And left you in a bad situation." Her eyes flashed to his face, and Tyler said, "He was my friend, but it's true, Skye."

She folded her arms over her chest, pushing the damp sweatshirt beneath her raincoat into her bare skin, which in turn made her shiver. "*Here's* the truth, Tyler—I'm still dealing with stuff. And until I'm done..." She had no idea how to finish the sentence, no idea how to tell him that as attractive as she found him, she was not hooking up with a bull rider—not even on a temporary basis—so she shrugged.

"Deal away, Skye. Just don't paint me as the bad guy."

"I'm not." To her surprise, she meant it. She no longer saw Tyler as a bad guy...but she did see him as dangerous, which might be worse in some ways. "You're my business partner."

My dangerous business partner.

She cleared her throat before tackling the hard part.

"Which means that we should probably act like partners, instead of manhandling one another."

"Manhandling?"

"Okay. Maybe that was a stretch." The rain started to pound on the porch roof, and small rivulets were running down the driveway. "No more kissing."

"Because…"

She pushed her wet hood back. Her hair was damp around the edges, sticking uncomfortably to her face. "It makes for an uneasy partnership."

And would continue to make for an uneasy partnership for long as she was who she was and Tyler was who he was.

"I think we need to keep an open mind, Skye."

The intensity of his expression made her insides tumble. "I don't think that's wise. I'm not ready to jump into anything. Especially not…with a friend of Mason's. We can't be…attracted."

His eyebrows lifted. "I don't think we have much of a choice."

Skye swallowed as an odd emotion stirred somewhere inside her as she tried to explain. "Since Mason died, I don't feel like I've had much of a choice in anything. I do have a choice here. I choose peace of mind." A gust of wind blasted over them, bringing the rain with it. "We should get out of the weather."

His mouth opened, as if to argue, then closed again. "Agreed."

He waited for a moment, as if wondering if she was going to invite him into her house. She couldn't do it. "I'll see you later."

He stepped back, teetering for a moment on the edge of the porch. Skye reached for him, but he got his balance before she could touch him and she dropped her hands. He forced a smile. "You can't hurt a bull rider."

She begged to differ, but kept the thought to herself.

Don't push things.

It was so hard not to. Tyler had spent his life pushing boundaries, but he wanted to get back out onto the road, so he was doing his best to stop doing whatever it was he was doing when his injuries started hurting instead of pushing through it. Not easy to do when he'd always pushed through the pain, but this was the first time he was looking at surgery, or maybe not finishing a season, so he needed to change his mind-set.

Again, no easy task, but Skye was helping. She was downright strict about what he could and could not do on her roof—even if technically it was their roof. Tyler had let her call the shots when she was around, and they finished the final side of the last roof that morning, before the rain.

Twilight was setting in by the time he left Skye's porch and headed for his trailer through the rain, still battling frustration. Mason had left a mess behind him, and Tyler was suffering the consequences.

Reality really sucked at times.

Yet another long evening stretched ahead of him, and he thought about calling his twin as he headed up the mucky path to his trailer. Instead he decided to head to town and see who was at the Shamrock. It was Friday night and there should be action there—any action was better than hanging in his trailer alone.

He showered in the tiny shower stall, wondering as he always did how a guy with some size on him would manage in such a small place. Not a worry of his. His body was about as lean as it could be. After he toweled off, he found a clean, albeit somewhat wrinkled shirt and decent jeans, and, since he was going out in public, he put on his good boots with the teal green uppers. Then he pulled his pant legs down over the boots so that no one could see the tops. It was the way things worked in his world. He knew about the green teal leather, and anyone who got him out of his pants would know about them.

He smiled grimly as he shrugged into a canvas vest. No one would be seeing his boots tonight. He wasn't in the mood for something quick and meaningless. Hadn't been for a while now.

The Shamrock was hopping when he got there. It didn't take him long to locate his bull-riding buddies—Cody, Trace Delaney and his cousin, Blaine. Even Jasper Hennessey was there, but he set his hat on his head as Tyler approached the group.

"Just leaving," he said, clapping Tyler on the good shoulder. "Do some howling for me tonight, okay?"

"You could stay and do your own."

Jasper gave his head a shake. "I don't get the same thrill out of it as I used to. I'm only here because the kids dragged me."

The "kids" were all well over legal age, with Cody being the youngest. Tyler smiled and wished Jasper a good night, then pulled out a chair.

"You should have seen Trace today," Cody said with a laugh. "Landed face-first in a pile of—" He abruptly stopped when Trace raised a finger in a mock warning.

"Sounds entertaining."

"When are you heading back out on the road?" Tyler

asked Trace after ordering two pitchers of beer from the server who cruised by.

"Annie and I leave day after tomorrow. She wanted to travel a little before I settle."

"Settle?" Tyler asked.

"It's my last season," Trace said. No one else at the table seemed surprised at the announcement.

"No kidding."

"Embracing my new life," he said. "I'm going to work for Jasper. Won't pay that much, but I'll be home at night."

"Congrats, man."

Tyler went on to ask Trace about his shoulder surgery, since he was looking at nearly the same operation, then after hearing the cold hard facts, he settled in for some drinking. Trace left not long after they finished their conversation, leaving him with Blaine and Cody.

The two bull riders kept the beer coming, but Tyler drank slowly, seemingly one to their two. Cody and Blaine both had family within walking distance of the Shamrock, while he would be sleeping in his truck if he didn't watch himself.

Cody was getting downright funny as he described the latest goings-on at the practice pen and gossiped about his fellow bull riders' love lives. Tyler made a mental note to keep his mouth quiet around Cody in the future and was still smiling at the kid's story about Jasper's wife coming to the practice pen and telling him off for not doing the laundry on "his" day when he became aware of someone coming to a stop close to his chair. He looked up, straight into Paige Andrews's very green eyes. He'd seen her and her friend Tiffani

Crenshaw when he'd first come in and had been glad that their table was on the opposite side of the room.

"Hello, Tyler."

"Paige." He tipped his hat back as Cody's chair scraped across the floor before he excused himself with a polite nod at Paige.

Tyler felt very much like telling the kid to come back, even if it meant being ribbed later, but the kid was already long gone, and Blaine was nowhere in sight, either.

Paige settled in the chair that Cody had just vacated. "How long will you be home?"

"A couple of weeks."

"And, obviously, home is Skye Larkin's ranch?"

He worked up an easy smile. "It is. We're partners in the ranch."

Paige's eyebrows rose. "How did that come about?"

Tyler leaned his elbows on the table. "Through a string of circumstances." He glanced down at his clasped hands for a moment, then back up at Paige, meeting her gaze dead on. Her mouth, which tilted up naturally at the corners, tilted even more.

"Tiffani has to leave soon. Why don't you join me for the rest of the evening?"

"Because I don't think that's a very good idea." If she wanted company, there were any number of guys in the bar who would be happy to oblige. She was pretty and polished and had an air of cool confidence that was extremely sexy. The problem was that she had a very hard time taking no for an answer, and that had ultimately been the answer Tyler had given her six months ago. It wasn't an answer she liked.

Paige gave a measured shrug. "Maybe at some point

in the future, then." She smiled at him as if it were only a matter of time until he came around to her way of thinking and gracefully rose to her feet. He thought about telling her that there wouldn't be a future time—that they'd dated and it hadn't worked—but kept his mouth shut.

Yes, they'd had some fun, but she wanted too much control—of everything. Tyler didn't mind compromise, but he wasn't interested in being managed...although he had to admit to kind of liking it when Skye managed him.

Paige sauntered back across the room to the table she shared with Tiffani, who'd been watching with interest, and then the two women picked up their purses and headed for the door. Tyler let out a long breath just as Cody came back to reclaim his chair.

"She's hot."

"Ask her out," Tyler suggested as he poured them both more beer.

Cody shook his head. "I know my limitations, man. That woman would eat me alive. Besides... I kind of like Angie."

Probably because they both enjoyed passing along good gossip. Tyler just smiled and lifted his drink in a salute before promising himself to watch his mouth around his friend. Cody was bad enough on his own, but if he passed things on to Angie with her connections to the beauty shop and café...watch out.

SKYE JERKED AWAKE as Tyler's pickup drove past her window, and then she settled back against her pillow, heart pounding. Not since Mason had been alive had someone driven in during the early morning hours.

She exhaled deeply and closed her eyes again.

No use. She was awake, but it was close to the time her alarm was set to go off. Since the bars closed at one o'clock, she could only imagine where he'd been until now.

You do not want to know.

Although a small part of her did. She wanted to know if he'd been doing what she'd been thinking about, then in turn wondered why such a thought made her feel jealous. She got out of bed and went into the bathroom, where she turned on the shower. She took her time making coffee, reading the news on her phone as she ate toast with jam and drank two cups of coffee. A normal morning…except that she kept wondering about Tyler.

When she let herself out of her house, she was surprised to see Tyler sitting on the steps of the granary, drinking a cup of coffee in the watery morning sun. She set her purse in her car, then crossed the driveway.

"Decided not to sleep?"

"I slept," he said.

"When?"

"After the bar closed. I climbed into my truck and got a whopping four hours." He took a drink of coffee. "I don't drive after drinking. No good ever comes of that."

"You're sober now?"

"Wasn't that drunk to begin with."

"Your eyes are red."

"Lack of sleep?" She shook her head and started for her car, but Tyler caught up with her before she'd gone more than a couple of steps. "Stop thinking the worst of me, Skye."

"I don't." The denial was automatic and not quite true. She did think the worst of him, and as time passed she was becoming convinced that she did it as self-protection mechanism.

"Yeah. You do." He pushed up the brim of his ball cap. "If you let me use your horse, I'll ride the summer pasture perimeter today."

"That sounds good," she said stiffly, even though she'd been looking forward to the ride. It had been a while since she'd been out. Life had kind of beat up on her for a while, and she'd pushed small things like riding and knitting to the side.

"Easier than borrowing a horse from the neighbor."

"Totally." She gave him a quick apologetic smile. "I have to get going."

"Come out with me tonight."

Skye stopped so fast that she almost left divots in the gravel at her feet. "What?" she asked, startled and half-convinced she'd misunderstood.

"I said, 'Come out with me.'"

"Like...out?"

"Yeah."

"Not like a...date?"

"Maybe."

She tilted her chin. "Weren't you listening yesterday when we talked?"

"It'll be a business date."

She frowned at him, wondering if he was messing with her, but he seemed totally sincere. "Where are we going on our business date?"

"The Shamrock."

"So it's a drinking business date."

"Kind of the Montana version of the three-martini lunch."

"I thought that was two-martini."

"We go big or go home here."

"No."

"Mason is gone, Skye. I'm here. I agree that it's not good practice between business partners, but we haven't exactly had a smooth business relationship thus far, have we?"

"Uh…no."

He smiled at her. Not the cocky bull rider smile, but the one that she'd seen only a handful of times when he let down his guard—as he was now. "Then we don't have much to muck up, do we?"

She hated a logical argument that made it all the easier to get herself into trouble. Skye kicked the gravel at her feet. "I should say no."

"But you aren't."

She gave a snort as she met his eyes. "Yes."

He cocked his head and asked cautiously, "Yes, you *are* saying no? Or yes, you're saying yes?"

"Ty…" It was the first time she'd ever used the shortened version of his name, and it felt oddly intimate coming off her tongue.

"Skye…" The rhyme made it possible for him to exactly mimic her tone. His expression became serious. "How long has it been since you went out and had fun, Skye?"

"You mean like cut-loose fun?"

"Yes."

"Believe it or not, I haven't felt like having that kind of fun. Life kind of smacked it out of me."

"Then we need to get you up to speed again."

"And you think you're the guy to do that?"

He gave her the cocky smile. "Kind of sure." Despite the attitude, she could see a trace of uncertainty in his expression. "Trust me, Skye."

Trust him. Oddly, at a gut level, she did. And it was time for a change in her life. Time to move on. She'd never expected Tyler Hayward to be the guy to help her out there, but why not?

"Fine. I'll have a business date with you—not a cut-loose date. We'll discuss our partnership and our goals for the future."

"Pick you up at seven?"

Chapter Twelve

What did one wear on a business date? Which really wasn't a business date, but she was pretending it was, and Tyler was playing along. That right there told her that Tyler Hayward wasn't the guy she'd thought he was.

Skye mentally flipped through her closet, which hadn't seen anything new in well over a year. What would she have worn if she and Mason had been going out to the Shamrock? As opposed to what would she wear when she went out as a single woman for the first time?

You are single.

Skye twisted the simple wedding band on her finger.

Not an easy thought, but an honest one. She was single and she was young. For the past year she'd stayed close to the ranch when she wasn't working, had turned down tentatively offered social invitations until they eventually dried up, and then it was just her and Jinx hanging out alone at night. And she'd been happy with that existence until Tyler had come into her life.

In just a few short weeks, things had changed due to finances, unforeseen circumstances and a stubborn, hard-to-manage bull rider.

And now she had nothing to wear…nothing that didn't bring back a boatload of memories anyway. She debated about asking Chloe if she could borrow one of her blingy tops, but she decided against it because she didn't want to answer questions. Yet. She'd be answering them soon enough. Gavin was a small town in every sense of the word. Just working one shift in the café earned her more gossip than she knew what to do with.

It was a good tip day, and as soon as Skye got off shift, she decided to splurge and buy something new. How comfortable would she feel in her old memory-laden clothing as she took this new step in her life?

Besides, she wanted something new. It had been a long, long time since she'd spent money on herself. She stopped by the new Western clothing boutique two blocks from the café and, after pricing things, decided she'd skip the new jeans and buy a fancy shirt. Then she saw the dresses on the sale rack. The first thing she pulled off the rack was a red sheath. Perfect to wear under a short denim jacket with boots. She had the jacket. She had the boots. Fifteen minutes later she had the dress, and then, on impulse, she walked into her favorite store, Annie Get Your Gun, on her way by.

Danielle Perry Adams looked up from where she stood behind the counter and smiled. "Hey, stranger."

"I think I just saw you a few days ago," Skye said with a frown.

"That was in your territory, at the café. I haven't seen you in the store since Christmas."

"Been pinching pennies."

Danielle came out from behind the counter. "Are you looking for another gift?"

"No. I'm looking for one of those big necklaces."

"A statement necklace. Lex just brought in some cool pieces. Do you want to see them?"

"Are they in my budget?"

"Why don't we take a look?" Danielle led the way to an antique table in the rear of the store where several silver and stone necklaces were tastefully arranged in a display of antique spurs.

"Wow. I don't even have to turn over a price tag…" Her eye caught a more delicate piece draped over a polished piece of sagebrush. "I like that one." It wasn't what she'd come in to buy. She'd been thinking funky. Something different. But the oddly shaped lapis stone set in silver on the simple chain spoke to her.

Danielle picked up the piece and turned it over. Skye looked at the price and nodded, pursing her lips together. It would take a couple of days of decent tips to pay herself back. Or she could pull another double next time Chloe had a doctor's appointment and not put the money in the mortgage fund.

She drew in a breath and said, "I'll take it."

Danielle smiled. "Shall I wrap it?"

Skye shook her head. "I think I'll wear it."

"I'll cut the tags for you." Danielle took the necklace and then pulled a pair of small scissors from beside the cash register. "Let me help you."

Skye lifted her hair, and Danielle fastened the necklace and then stood back. "I know I say this all the time in the course of my day, but Skye…that necklace is gorgeous on you. The stone and your eyes are almost the same color."

Skye touched the stone. "Thank you." She dug into

her purse and pulled out a wad of small bills. "I hope you don't mind me paying you in tips."

"I could use the small bills," Danielle said with an easy smile as Skye smoothed out the bills. "Everyone from out of town seems to pay with a hundred-dollar bill. I get tired of dashing to the bank."

Skye's stomach was tight as she left the store—she'd spent money on herself, and she was moving forward into uncharted territory life-wise. She took a deep breath and told herself to get over it. Life went on. The ranch wouldn't fail because she'd spent forty dollars on a necklace that she loved. It had been a long, long time since she'd bought anything she loved. Now she had a dress and a necklace. More than that, she had an occasion to wear them.

And she was darned well going to enjoy herself while she did so.

Ty wasn't certain what exactly had prompted him to ask Skye out early that morning, because it certainly hadn't been on his list of things to do that day. Maybe it was because of the way she'd been looking at him, as if he were something that both aggravated and attracted her. Maybe it was because he honestly thought a night out would do her good. Whatever the reason, when Skye came out of the house that evening and crossed the driveway to his freshly washed and vacuumed truck, he was glad he'd made the move. She looked both grimly determined and wildly uncertain, and he knew that this was a huge thing for her—her first date since losing Mason. A business date, of course, because a real date would have been too threatening. It was common knowledge that one did not get involved with one's business partner, but Tyler had made a career out of bucking expectations.

Whatever happened, he was going to make certain Skye had a good time. After calling around, he'd managed to get together a mellower crew than usual. Trace had found a sitter, so he was bringing his new wife, Annie. Cody was bringing Angie who he promised wouldn't get drunk and dance on the pool table as his previous girlfriend had done. Blaine was supposed to show, but he was coming alone. Tyler had given him a heads-up about Cody and Angie being part of the group, but Blaine had assured him the breakup had been both mutual and amicable. Blaine was always mellow, so Tyler wasn't concerned about him. He halfway wished his brother, Jess, could have been there, because Skye felt comfortable with him, but another part of him said no, he did not want to share.

"You look good," Skye said as she approached. Well, he had ironed his white shirt and dug out his newest jeans.

"As do you." He was not being polite. She wore a slim red dress under a short jean jacket that made him want to swallow when he first saw her. And the tops of her boots—red—did show, unlike his. He smiled as she got closer. "I like the necklace." The blue stone looked good on the red, but more than that, it seemed to reflect the color of her eyes.

She touched it self-consciously, then let her hand drop. "You realize this is my first time out in a long time."

"It's just the Shamrock. We're meeting people there for our business date."

"And I haven't been single in about six years." She

held his gaze as she spoke, and Tyler reached up to lightly brush his knuckles across her cheek.

"Yeah. I know. Let's just go have fun. We can come home super early if you want."

She smiled a little. "Thank you. And please realize that if I don't make small talk as we drive, it's because I'm really bad at small talk."

"We'll discuss ranch business as we drive." He opened the door for her, and she climbed into the cab of the truck, hiking her dress up over truly beautiful thighs in order to make the big step up. She smoothed her dress down and looked straight ahead as he shut the door, tipping up her chin as if mentally girding herself for the challenge ahead.

He blew out a breath as he walked around the back of the truck. He was not going to screw this night up. No, he was not.

SKYE FELT AS if a spotlight was on her when she walked into the Shamrock with Tyler. Heads literally turned. Not that many heads, but enough to tell her that no one expected her to be there, wearing a new dress and jewelry, on the arm of Tyler Hayward.

She felt like announcing that it was a business date and nothing more, but that was so not true. It was a turning point. Her first date since her husband's death, and it was with a guy she'd once ducked behind trees and bookshelves to avoid.

A guy who now had his hand comfortably resting at her elbow as he guided her to the bar.

"Hey, folks," Gus Hawkins said with an easy grin. "What can I get for you?"

Tyler glanced down at Skye, and there was something in the way he looked at her that made her throat go dry.

Business date. Business date. And there would be more people joining them. She was safe. For now.

"What would you like?"

"Beer would be nice." And would perhaps help calm her overactive nerves.

Tyler ordered two drafts, then picked up both glasses as Skye led the way to a table toward the back where it felt more private.

"Feel well hidden now?" Tyler asked,

"More hidden anyway." She pulled her glass closer. "This is a big step for me."

"I know."

Surprisingly, she believed that he did know. "I feel self-conscious."

"And like you're cheating on your late husband?"

She met his eyes. "A little."

He reached out and covered her fingers with his, gave them a quick squeeze, then pulled his hand away again. Skye took hold of her glass but did not drink. Instead she took a moment to study the man sitting across the table from her. His face was entirely healed now, but for how long? How many times had Mason left home pretty and come back swollen and broken?

Did she want to get back into that again?

As a bull rider's wife, she knew fear, and she knew prayer. Ultimately she'd relied on the latter along with a healthy dose of optimism. Things would be okay. And as far as bull riding went, they had been.

Tyler sipped his beer, allowing Skye her silence. Mason had never been comfortable with prolonged silence, and she'd assumed without thinking that Tyler was the same. But no. Instead of forcing conversation, he seemed content to give Skye time to decide her next step. That, too, surprised her.

So what was she going to do now that she was out with an attractive man whom three months ago she would have refused to share a table with? A man she'd once thought was to blame for a lot of her misfortune?

She had no idea what she was going to do, and she was surprisingly okay with that. They were out for a drink. There wasn't even a dinner involved. There could have been, but she nixed it, and Tyler had gone along with her wishes without an argument.

Imagine that… Tyler Hayward without an argument.

Was she getting in over her head?

No…she wasn't even knee-deep yet, and, if she took care, she wouldn't slip into deep water.

"A penny for your thoughts?"

"Fat chance," Skye murmured before meeting his gaze. "I told you I wasn't a great conversationalist."

He smiled at her. "Maybe you can pretend that we're on the roof in a storm."

"Maybe." She pressed her lips together thoughtfully. "This is harder than I thought it would be."

"We can leave anytime you want." Tyler reached for her hand, when a commotion started at the door and they both looked that way. Gus was already at the door, coolly suggesting that the rowdy couple find another place to drink.

Skye tucked her hands into her lap before looking back at Tyler. "I didn't expect to feel this conflicted."

"Things take time."

"It's been eighteen months."

"Everyone has their own schedule. Why don't I take you home?"

She shook her head and picked up her drink. "I have to start somewhere, and I may as well start by being out with someone who gets it."

"Bet you never thought you'd say those words."

"No," she said with a small laugh. "I never did." She set the drink down. "I like you, Ty. And that scares me to death."

"Because you know it's the first step toward being forever smitten?" he teased.

"Exactly." She picked her drink back up.

"It's a problem I have."

"I bet you do."

This time when he reached for her hand, she didn't pull hers away. "I'm not asking for anything, Skye, except for an open mind. Don't talk yourself in or out of something for the wrong reason."

"What," she asked softly, "might be considered a wrong reason?"

"Guilt. Fear." He waggled his eyebrows. "Lust."

Skye nearly spit out her drink. She dabbed a napkin at her mouth. "Unfair."

He grinned back unrepentantly. "Hey... I gotta be me."

Skye laughed in spite of herself, and after that the mood lightened. She finished her drink and ordered another as Tyler talked about life on the road, life as a twin. Life in general. He seemed happy to carry the conversational burden, until Skye relaxed enough to lean her elbows on the table and ask, "Do you see us becoming friends?"

"Like you and Jess are friends?" He shook his head.

Skye moistened her lips. "Then what?"

"I don't know." He spoke with an honest intensity that made Skye's cheeks begin to feel warm. Not from embarrassment or self-consciousness but rather from raw awareness. "But whatever it is, it'll be something mutually agreed upon."

"That sounds very...civilized."

"For a rough-and-ready bull rider?"

"Something like that," she admitted.

"You compare me to Mason."

It was a statement, not a question, and it gave Skye pause. "It's that apparent?"

"It's logical. We were friends in the same profession."

Skye lightly cleared her throat. "I can't help it."

"I'm a different kind of guy than Mason was."

She didn't ask how, maybe because she was afraid of the answer.

Oh, deep water, here I come...

Tyler suddenly raised his chin and Skye turned in her chair to see a group of familiar people crossing the room—Angie and her new bull-riding beau, Cody, as well as Trace and Annie Delaney.

Tyler raised a hand to greet them, then shifted his chair so that it was closer to hers, thus freeing up space for the newcomers.

Skye smiled and said hello as people settled in chairs, then jumped as Tyler touched her knee under the table. He leaned close and said, "We'll continue this business conversation later?"

Skye held his gaze for a moment, wondering if he'd made her jump on purpose because she wasn't in a position to call him on it. Or had he simply wanted to touch her?

She waited for him to casually raise his beer before reaching out to settle her hand on his knee. He coughed and she smiled a little before pulling her hand away and turning toward Angie to ask how she liked school.

REALLY, SKYE?

Tyler had almost choked on his beer when Skye touched his leg. The touching, in itself, was no big deal, except that it was Skye, making physical contact with him of her own accord. Maybe it was payback for him touching her...or maybe it wasn't.

He wasn't certain, but he was looking forward to getting the answer later that evening. In the meantime, Skye pretty much focused on everyone at the table, except for him. When Grady and Lex showed up they scooted their chairs even closer and Tyler slid his arm along the back of Skye's chair. She turned to look at him, her expression making him feel like a junior high kid who'd been caught doing the arm-around-the-girl-while-yawning move.

He gave her a mock frown and lightly caressed her bare arm with his fingertips. A shiver went through her and her eyes widened ever so slightly. Then she turned back to Angie, her hair sliding over his arm like a smooth silken sheet.

Tyler felt his body stir at the sensual contact, then told his body to knock it off. Not the time or place and he was thirty freaking years old. He continued to stroke Skye's arm ever so lightly and she did not move away. Nor did she move closer—not until she leaned in to say, "This is not the way I do business."

"We might have to discuss your technique."

"Fat chance," she whispered sweetly.

"We'll see," he murmured back. He looked up then, caught Grady studying him with a slight frown and had the craziest feeling that his fellow bull rider wanted to offer him some advice. He looked away. He was doing okay, considering the circumstances. He'd gotten Skye out on a date, hadn't he? She'd touched his leg. Major headway.

The group broke up early. Trace and Grady and their ladies had duties at home and since Tyler had a feeling that Cody and Angie were itching to ramp up their evening, he and Skye left with the married crowd. The couples went their separate ways in the parking lot and after opening Skye's door for her and helping her into the truck, Tyler walked around and got into his own side.

Skye sat close to the window, her face turned slightly away from him, as if being alone with him without the protection of a crowd was suddenly too intimate.

What happened to the woman who'd patted his leg under the table?

She certainly wasn't there in the truck with him.

Tyler did Skye a favor and left her alone in her thoughts on the short drive out of town to the ranch.

Once they'd parked, he'd half expected her to bolt from the truck, but instead she opened her door and made her way to the ground, taking care not to tear her tight-ish red dress. A dress that didn't cry out "business date."

Tyler walked Skye to her door, maintaining the silence until she'd put her key into the lock. Then he reached out to put his hand on top of hers, stopping her from turning the key. Her startled gaze jerked up to his and he saw color stain her cheeks. He eased back, dropped his hand.

"I was just wondering if tonight was…okay."

"Tonight was fun." She seemed sincere, but still distant.

"What's wrong?"

She glanced down ever so briefly before raising her gaze first to his mouth, then to his eyes. She moistened her lips. "As we spoke about before…a lot of firsts."

Tyler tipped his chin up and looked down at her. "Have you ever heard of fear fantasies, Skye?"

She gave her head a slow shake.

"It's when you think about all the things that could go wrong and worry about them, just as if they had gone wrong. Your body reacts accordingly."

"But…isn't it a good thing to anticipate problems? Be prepared?"

"Yes. But it isn't a good idea to obsess over things that could happen, but haven't."

Her eyebrows drew together and he abandoned his intention of keeping his hands off her. Gripping her lightly by the shoulders, he moved a step closer, bringing her close enough to feel the heat of her body, breathe in her wonderful scent, but not close enough for their bodies to touch. "Skye," he said patiently, "you can be prepared, but you also need to understand that you can't control the future. You can kind of control the moment you're in…unless, of course, you're on a bull. Then it's a totally different thing."

She bit her lip, fought the smile. He smiled at her

and it broke through. She shook her head one more time and then leaned it on his chest.

"You drive me crazy."

"In a good way?"

"For the most part."

He reached down and tipped up her chin, then took her lips in a soft, sweet kiss. It was all he would allow himself, because he was not going to mess this up. Skye's lips clung to his, making it all the more difficult to pull away. Somehow he did.

"I will not push things, Skye. Slow and steady. No fast moves."

"You make me sound like a green colt."

He smiled a little. "No. Just someone who needs some practice living in the moment without imagining awful consequences in the future."

Live in the moment.

The words had become Skye's mantra, and now, as she put the finishing touches on the lasagna she was making for dinner—hopefully to be shared with Tyler, if she could find him to invite him—she repeated them again. She could control the moment. She couldn't control the future.

She went to the window and peered out across the field where Tyler had taken the four-wheeler to check on cattle in a far pasture. No sign of him. She picked up the heavy pan and put it into the oven.

They'd fallen into a routine of sorts after their date at the Shamrock. During the day, they kept things businesslike. Tyler did his thing—the fencing and the maintenance—and she did hers—the feeding and the cow management. They didn't spend that much time together—they were at work, after all—but in the evening, Tyler would knock on her door, invite her out for a walk. Or a drive to town. And sometimes she invited him to dinner, as she was doing tonight.

They moved forward cautiously, both ultra-aware of the fact that Tyler would be leaving soon, and sometimes he would kiss her good-night before leaving her to go to his trailer. A gentle kiss that left her wanting more.

Part of his plan? She thought not. He was honestly trying not to spook her. To allow her time to come to terms with the fact that attraction didn't mean disaster… and that she could trust him.

Skye was going a little crazy with it all. She wanted more. She was afraid of more. She didn't want a fling, but she didn't want commitment. But she wanted Tyler.

And that seemed like a good way to totally screw up her life.

Live in the moment.

A truck pulled into the driveway, and Skye wiped her hands on a towel as she walked to the door. The guy was already halfway up the walk, carrying a vase of daisies and small rosebuds.

"Who're they from?" she asked, even though she could think of only one person who would send her flowers.

The guy shrugged. "Read the card."

She did and smiled. Flowers. Other than for her proms, she'd never received flowers. Mason hadn't been a flowers type of guy, but apparently Tyler was.

Who would have thought?

And what did she do about it?

Say thank you, and continue as usual. The only problem was that she wasn't certain about what usual entailed. They couldn't continue as they were indefinitely—but Tyler was leaving, so they could continue until then... unless she gave in and did what she really wanted to do. With him.

She was afraid—not of him, but of herself. Of needing someone and losing them.

But she couldn't stop thinking about the guy and... well...possibilities.

AT SIX O'CLOCK, after the lasagna had been out of the oven for almost half an hour, she started to suspect that something was wrong. Tyler was rarely this late getting back to the ranch when he worked the perimeters. At six thirty, as it was growing dark, she kicked off her heels and slipped into her barn boots. She grabbed the flashlight off the charger on the wall, pulled a hoodie on over her dress and headed outside, wishing she'd acted earlier. Something wasn't right.

She was tired of things not being right and she was tired of knee-jerk fear reactions, but if something had happened to him...

When she reached the middle of the driveway, she stopped as a flash of light in the middle of the pasture caught her eye and relief slammed into her. The light came bobbing closer and Skye realized it was from a cell phone. Tyler was almost to the pasture gate by the time she reached it.

"Did you get my flowers?" he asked as she undid the latch. His crooked smile almost did her in.

"I did. What happened?"

"The four-wheeler ran out of gas."

Her eyes widened, more out of anger than relief now

that she knew he was safe. Out of gas? "Damn it, Ty, I was scared to death—"

He reached for her and pulled her closer, bringing his hands up to frame her face before leaning down to touch his forehead to hers. She let out a ragged sigh as she felt the reassuring contact. He was close and he was okay. She took hold of his upper arms, felt the tightly bunched muscles beneath her palms. "Sorry," she murmured.

"The last thing I ever want to do is scare you, Skye. It was a stupid mistake. I was in a hurry this morning… I'm sorry."

Skye nodded against his forehead. "It's okay. I'm… easily triggered." But then, when she thought he was going to kiss her, he stepped back, dropped his hands.

She hated losing the connection.

Hated that she was afraid to move forward with anything. *Really, Skye? You can't go after what you want…what you* need*?*

He took her hand, and together they crossed the driveway to her porch, where he stopped. "I'm a mess," he said.

He was pretty muddy. Skye looked him over, then gave her head a shake. "I guess you need a shower."

"Yeah." He leaned in and gave her a quick kiss, before turning to start down the steps.

"Where are you going?" Her voice didn't sound like her own.

He shot her a frowning look over his shoulder. "To shower?"

She sucked up her courage, then gestured toward her front door with her head. "Would you like to use mine?"

The emotions that chased across Tyler's face would have been comical under other circumstances, but Skye didn't feel like laughing. She waited, her heart beating too hard, too fast, until he said, "Are you sure, Skye?"

She gave a small nod. "I've never been surer."

SKYE WAS SURE, but she was also nervous. Tyler could feel her pulse racing beneath his fingers as he took her hands and ran his thumb over her wrists. Too soon? He didn't want to push things.

She pulled a breath in over her teeth before pulling her hands out of his and Tyler felt a swell of disappointment, coupled with acceptance. Half a heartbeat later her arms were around his neck and her lips were on his, demanding what he'd been holding back for so long.

Tyler met her kiss, asking for more. Skye was where she belonged, in his arms, her soft curves pressing into him. He pushed one hand up into her soft hair as his other slid lower, over her firm bottom. Perfect. Utterly perfect. He deepened the kiss, bringing her even more tightly against him. He wanted her and now she was aware of just how much.

"I really do need a shower," he murmured against her mouth.

"So do I."

"How big is your shower?" he asked in a low voice, his hands running gently up and down over her back.

She smiled slowly. "Big enough."

And it was—big enough to allow the two of them to get wet, soap up, slowly explore one another's bodies. Before things got out of hand—just barely—Tyler cranked the water off and opened the glass door, allowing Skye to exit before him. Then he took a towel and slowly dried her off.

Her eyes went closed and her breath caught, but he continued to wipe away the moisture that clung to her perfect body.

He sensed that she was still nervous…but so was he.

Skye opened her eyes and held out her hand for the towel. "My turn."

"I…"

"Shh." She put the towel on his head and briskly dried his hair, smiling a little as she did so, but the smile faded as she began working the towel over his shoulders, his chest, his stomach…

Tyler was barely aware of moving, but the towel dropped to the floor as he swung Skye up into his arms, cradling her against his chest. There was so much he wanted to say, but more than that he wanted to act. To show Skye exactly how much he cared for her.

Skye gave a gasp at the intimate contact, then wound her arms more tightly around his neck. She touched his lips with hers before whispering, "My room is straight across the hall."

Chapter Thirteen

In less than forty-eight hours, Tyler would be on the road again. His shoulder felt good, probably because Skye had been nuts about not letting him use it over the past several weeks, and he hoped that he could finish the season, bring in some more money.

The ranch buildings were roofed. The cattle moved. The fence was fixed as well as he could fix it, and it was definitely good enough to keep the cattle—and a donkey—in until he got back, unless of course the cattle decided they really wanted out. Then there would probably be no stopping them. Blaine had already agreed to be on call if Skye needed help on the ranch, although he pointed out that she'd run the ranch just fine without him or Tyler until a few weeks ago. Tyler agreed, but he felt better knowing that someone was there when he and his brother were not around.

For the first time in his life, he wasn't practically jumping out of his skin in anticipation of getting back out onto the circuit. Yes, he wanted to ride, but he didn't like leaving Skye behind.

It was only for a matter of a few weeks, and then he'd have a break and be able to come home for a few days.

Home. Wow.

Things were moving rapidly, but he was good with that. He'd cared for Skye forever, and now it seemed as if she was allowing herself to care for him. They now shared her bed, and more and more of his belongings had made their way into her house.

They lived together and worked together and it seemed to be working. They didn't talk about the future, but Tyler had faith they were on the same page... that they were working toward a commitment.

She came out of the house and crossed the driveway to where he waited in the truck, looking great in slim-fitting jeans and a scoop-neck blue T-shirt, carrying a covered bowl for the potluck they were attending. The Founders Day picnic was a big community event, but he hadn't been to one in years, since he was usually on the road during the weekend it was held. Skye had told him she'd missed only one—last year's.

The parking lot was packed when they pulled in, and after he found parking, Skye hurried across the lot to put her pasta salad on the table with the other side dishes. Trace hailed Tyler from a table at the edge of the park, and as soon as Skye rejoined him, he took her hand and they crossed over to join the group at the same time that Grady Owen and his bride, Lex, approached from the opposite direction.

Lex had always scared Tyler a little. She was about as no-nonsense as a woman came and called things the way she saw them. Grady was smitten by her, which was funny, since for the longest time he'd considered her a sworn enemy. Very much as Skye had considered him to be the enemy. Funny how things worked out sometimes, even though he and Skye were still in the very early stages of nailing something down between them.

Trace and Annie's twins raced by with several kids in hot pursuit, one of them swinging a small lariat. Tyler gathered from the twins' laughs and whinnies that they were wild horses and the other kids were trying to capture them. Good game. He remembered playing it a time or two himself back in the day.

"Be careful!" Trace yelled to the kids as the boy swinging the rope tripped over the end and went down. He jumped back to his feet, and the chase continued.

"I wish I could bottle that energy," Annie said as the kids circled the swing set.

"You'd be rich," Skye agreed, taking a seat beside her.

Tyler sat next to Grady, and they discussed the standings in the tour as well as Tyler's chances of gaining enough points to make the finals.

"I'd like to final," he admitted, "but I think that's unlikely. Mostly I'd like to earn enough to cover my road expenses and the surgery, so I can start fresh next year."

"You mean fresh in April," Grady said.

It would take that long to recover, so yes, that was what he meant. And while he was recovering, he'd work the ranch. Not exactly a win-win, since surgery was involved, but close. He glanced over at Skye, who was deep in conversation with Lex and Annie, and smiled to himself. She was more relaxed than he'd ever seen her, and when she glanced up unexpectedly and caught him studying her, she smiled a little, then focused back on Lex.

Things were good. He hoped they stayed good.

SKYE HAD RARELY ever stayed at the Founders Day celebration after the cleanup, but this year there was a dance and fireworks and she wanted to stay. Tyler would be gone in less than two days, and she was going to indulge in her fantasy world for a little longer.

Was it really fantasy?

More like idyllic, and that would change as real life happened. If she and Tyler continued their slow process toward a relationship, they would eventually argue and learn to work out compromises. Life wouldn't be all roses…but it was all roses at the moment, and there wasn't one thing wrong with enjoying the present without worrying about the future.

Lex and Annie worked with her to clear the tables, placing the bowls on a long table in the kitchen facility where the owners could claim them before they left. When Skye came out of the kitchen with a bucket of warm water and a sponge to wash the tables, she caught sight of Tyler close to where the band was setting up, talking to Paige.

"I don't like her," Lex said as she came to join Skye in table-washing detail. There was no question whom she was talking about, since she gestured in the direction of Paige and Tyler with her chin.

Skye gave her a surprised look, but maybe it wasn't all that surprising. Lex didn't make friends easily. "Why's that?"

"Gut instinct."

Tyler smiled briefly at Paige then and turned and walked back to where Trace and his twins were sitting.

"She wants our ranch account for her new business."

"Just the account?" Lex asked.

"Well, no," Skye confessed. "But it's a small town

and exes have to see one another, and I don't think Ty's in the market." The important thing was that no matter where they were in their relationship, she trusted Tyler. He'd never lied to her—if anything he told her more truth than she wanted to hear. She needed to improve her breeding program—her fields were in rotten shape—and Vanessa was not the sweet goose Skye thought she was.

"Yeah. I think you're right there." Lex shot a look at Tyler. "He's as nailed down as I've ever seen him. Good work."

"Thanks," she said drily. She and Tyler had agreed to keep their budding relationship under wraps, but Cody had talked to Angie, who'd talked to the world, and there was now no such thing as being under wraps.

"No problem."

Skye and Lex finished the tables and then dumped the water. "I'm heading back out," she said as two guys came in with fresh black trash bags to reline the kitchen garbage cans.

"Tell Grady I'll be out shortly."

"Will do."

But when Skye started toward the table where Trace and Grady sat with Cody and Angie, who'd driven down from Missoula for the weekend, Tyler was gone.

"He's in the parking lot," Angie said before Skye could ask his whereabouts. "Talking to Paige." She gave Cody a tight-lipped sidelong look that made Skye's insides shift uneasily.

Things suddenly felt awkward at the table, as all eyes shifted toward Angie and then away again, and it appeared as if everyone was in on a deep, dark secret. What the heck?

Skye forced a smile and turned to head back to the kitchen, thinking she'd find Tyler later, when he was done talking to Paige in the parking lot. She'd only gone a couple of steps when she heard Cody ask Angie why she hadn't keep her mouth shut.

"I don't want that…thing…to happen to her again," Angie muttered in her quietest voice, which wasn't quiet at all.

It was all Skye could do not to turn on her heel and march back to the small group to discover what that "thing" was, but she continued her forward path. She'd talk to Angie later. Or better yet, she'd talk to Tyler, who was coming toward her from the direction of the parking lot. Paige's brand-new car backed out of a parking space and roared past them, out of the lot.

"What was that about?" Skye asked as Tyler looped an arm around her shoulders.

"I told her we weren't going to use her services." He gave her a look. "She might be good at what she does, but too much potential for complications."

"Must be rough being irresistible."

"A burden," he agreed. As he steered them toward the table where the bull riders sat, Skye slowed her steps. "Is something wrong?"

"I don't know."

"What does that mean?"

She shifted her position so that she was facing him. The uneasy feeling had yet to abate, and she decided that maybe an answer or two was in order. "Do you know of any secret thing that could happen to me… again?"

"What?"

"When you were in the parking lot with Paige,

Angie whispered something to Cody about not wanting that thing to happen to me again."

Tyler's gaze instantly jerked over to the bull riders' table, and she saw Cody give a small shrug. The knot in her stomach tightened. There was something she didn't know. Paige. Tyler. The "thing."

Her lips parted as a wild idea struck her. Crazy thought. It couldn't be.

"What don't I know?" she demanded.

His expression clouded, and she could see that he was fighting to find a response—one that she would find palatable.

"Tyler...explain this to me."

The look he gave her was both dark and pained. He shook his head. "It would be better if we just went home."

"Better for whom?"

He didn't answer. Skye glanced behind them, saw the three bull riders and Angie staring at them as if waiting for the aftermath of the events just set into motion. She looked back at Tyler, her stomach so tight that it was all she could do to hold nausea at bay as her theory continued to form.

It couldn't be.

"Tell me," she repeated.

He looked past her. "Not here." Tyler reached down to take her hand and interlace his fingers with hers. "Let's go."

Skye stood frozen for a moment and then nodded. They walked to his truck, and as always, Tyler opened the door for her. She climbed in but could see by Tyler's set expression that he wasn't about to discuss anything until they got back to the ranch.

It was not a long drive home, but tonight it felt never-ending. Angie hadn't been talking gambling. If she had, Tyler would have told her back in the parking lot.

By the time Tyler parked next to the barn, Skye's heart was beating as if she'd just run a couple of fast miles. He turned off the ignition and shifted in the seat so that he was half facing her.

"Yes or no, Tyler...did Mason cheat on me?" His mouth was a hard flat line that gave no sign of budging. "Tell me."

"Yes."

Arrow to the heart.

She couldn't breathe. Couldn't talk. Couldn't cry. She was...frozen.

She never suspected. Never, ever, ever. And how stupid did that make her?

"Skye."

She blinked at Tyler. "Who knows?" she asked lowly. "Does everyone know?"

"No."

"How did *you* know?"

"Because he wasn't that good at sneaking around."

"So...anyone who was on the circuit with him..." She swallowed, unable to finish the sentence.

Tyler stretched his arm along the seat, let his fingertips brush her shoulder, but she jerked away from his touch. "Grady, Trace and Cody are the only people in Gavin who know."

"And that explains Angie."

"Cody must have told her."

Skye closed her eyes, drew in a painful breath. This was close to how she'd felt when the sheriff's deputy had come to her house eighteen months ago with the unthinkable news about her husband. Very, very close.

"I know you're hurting."

Her eyes came open. "You have no concept. My entire relationship with my dead husband was a lie."

"Not all of it."

"Oh yeah? What part was real? The part where I trusted him? The part where I thought he had integrity?"

Tyler had no answer to that. She could see that he wanted to touch her, and she hoped beyond hope that he didn't. If he did, she would shatter. As it was, her skin seemed to burn and her throat was closing, but tears…there were no tears. Mason deserved no tears.

"He—"

"Do *not* tell me that he loved me." Skye clamped her teeth together then, so tightly that it seemed a miracle that they didn't crack and break.

"Let me stay with you, Skye."

She stared at him. Company? Now? No freaking way. She reached for the door handle and jerked it open. "No."

He flattened his mouth again, as if afraid that words she didn't want to hear were somehow going to escape. She shut the door and marched around the front of the truck and up the walk to her house. Once inside she snapped on the porch light but didn't bother with the interior light. Darkness. It was crowding her soul, so why not welcome it? Revel in it.

She sank down onto the sofa and sat, numbly staring across the room as her eyes adjusted to minimal light.

Her husband, her trusted husband, had lied to her.

And Tyler had, too. And…so had everyone else who

knew and didn't tell her. How stupid had she looked? The supportive wife who managed the ranch. Did extra duty so that her husband could follow his dreams.

She gathered a pillow to her middle, squeezed it hard, then threw it across the room, jumping a mile when a light rap sounded on the door. Without pausing to think, Skye jumped to her feet, crossed the room and yanked the door open.

"What?" she demanded.

"I don't have to go tomorrow."

She gaped at him through the semidarkness. "Why would I want you to stay?"

His chin jerked as if she'd just struck him. She couldn't help that. "Skye—"

"Why didn't you tell me?"

"Because there was no reason to tell you. Nothing could be changed or fixed. How would knowing have helped anything?" He took a step closer. "How is it helping now?"

"I'll tell you how it's helping," Skye said. "It's helping me understand that I can't trust my own instincts. That I don't know what I think I do. And that things that seem right can be very, very wrong."

He lifted his hands, as if to pull her into his embrace, and she took a step back. "Don't touch me."

"All right."

"I want…no, *I need*…to be alone."

"I understand."

"And I want the ranch to myself. When you come back on break, we'll talk. But tomorrow… I don't want to see you before you leave."

"Right." There was a clip to his voice now, as if he was also getting angry.

"I'm going to bed." She took hold of the door, and Tyler was wise enough to simply step back and allow her to close it.

Once the door was shut, Skye waited until she heard Tyler's boots head down the porch steps. That was when she felt the liquid fire running down her cheeks, dripping onto her chest.

Tears ran like rain, and she did nothing to stop the flow. She was a mess. Her life was a mess.

How was she ever supposed to trust herself or anyone else again?

Chapter Fourteen

Tyler paced through his trailer, unable to sleep. Skye's kitchen lights had come on not long after she'd shut the door on him and had yet to go off. What was she doing?

It was killing him to have to hang back and let her deal with Mason's betrayal on her own, even though logic told him that was the only way she could deal. What he hadn't expected was that she would lash out at him.

How was he supposed to head out on tour with things like they were? But he had to go. She needed time. He needed to make some money. She said they'd talk when he got back, and he was going to hold her to that, even though he hated the thought of her dealing with this alone.

Why couldn't Angie—and Cody—have kept their mouths shut? He was having a hard time tamping down his anger. Neither of them meant Skye any harm, but...

Tyler finally fell asleep sprawled on his small sofa sometime after 2:00 a.m. When he woke up, it was daylight and Skye's truck was gone. He shoved his feet into his boots and headed outside. The animals were fed, and the gray cat was sunning himself near the barn. He went back to his trailer and sat on the step. He didn't have to leave to catch his flight to Portland until after Skye got home from shift, and he was waiting until the last possible moment. Yeah, she wanted to be left alone, but he had a few things he wanted to say before heading out on the road.

Things he had to say.

He loaded his truck, checked everything on the ranch he could think to check, paced his trailer. Waited.

When Skye's usual arrival time came and went, he paced more. It was close to the time when he had to leave to catch his flight in Butte when he called the diner and asked what time Skye had left.

She'd left two hours before her shift was over. Chloe had covered for her. Tyler hung up, his gut tense with worry, when he heard the sound of her truck. He grabbed his keys and headed to the door. If the traffic was with him, he might still make the flight. Skye was getting out of the truck when he came out the door.

"Why are you still here?" she asked.

"I was worried about you." She looked sideways as if it pained her to hear that answer. He crossed the distance between them. "Nothing has changed between us, Skye."

Her eyes narrowed as if she couldn't believe he'd either said that or believed it.

"Things have changed with me, Tyler."

"How so?"

"Have you ever been betrayed?"

"I didn't betray you."

She gave him a look that clearly said she wasn't so certain about that before saying, "That wasn't the question."

Fine. He'd answer the question. "Not in a big way."

Skye pushed her hands into her pockets, the way she did when she was stressed. "If you ever had been, you'd understand that it makes you question everything."

"You don't need to question me, Skye."

"I don't know that."

He took a couple of paces closer, stopping when she gave him a warning look. "You do know that. I love you."

Her chin jerked up. "Don't."

But he did. He came forward and put his hands on her stiff shoulders. If anything, they stiffened even more. He hung on anyway, bringing his face closer to hers as he said, "I. Love. You. I understand that you don't want to hear it, but you need to know it before I leave." He let go of her and took a step back.

"Mason said he loved me, too. You saw how that turned out."

Anger flashed, catching him off guard. He sucked in a breath before saying in a deadly voice, "Don't *ever* put me in the same class as Mason. I did not make him gamble, I did not make him cheat and I'm in no way like him." He looked away, then brought his gaze back to clash with hers. Yeah, she was hurting. Lashing out. Well, he was starting to smart a little, too. "For the record, I hate that you would lump us together."

"Mason lied to me, you lied to me—" He started to cut her off, but she raised a finger in a warning gesture. "By omission, but it still feels like betrayal."

"So what now?"

"Things go back to the way they used to be. When our lives were very much separate."

"And you didn't have to take any risks?"

"If you were me, would you take risks?" Before he

could answer, she said, "Risks are not working for me. I want my nice, solitary life where no one slips a knife between my ribs when I'm not looking."

"And just like that, we're done?"

"No, Tyler. We're not done. We're business partners."

"And that's all?"

She gave a nod, and her voice was crisp and cold as she said, "Do not ask for more."

TYLER CAUGHT THE tour in New Mexico, where he had an okay ride. The bull he'd drawn wasn't the meanest bucker in the bunch, and even though he'd ridden for eight, his score didn't put him in the money. His shoulder had held up, though, so he was glad he'd followed doctor's orders and taken the time off—at least in the sense of having healed his body. As far as his personal life went, well, that was about as screwed up as it could get.

Should he have told Skye about Mason?

Why inflict pain when it wasn't necessary? Why destroy memories and the illusion of trust? He might have been wrong, but it still killed him to think of Skye's expression, which was freeze-framed into his brain, when she'd figured out what Angie had meant. What had been the chances of Skye ever finding out? Before the Founders Day celebration, before Cody had taken up with Angie, he would have said close to zero.

After Albuquerque, he caught a ride with another bull rider, Caiden Craig—aka CC—first to Phoenix, then to Bakersfield. Both of those rides were good, and he earned some money in Bakersfield. The next leg started in Denver, moved on to Salt Lake City, then Billings and Spokane, but he had three days before Denver—enough time to fly home, get his truck and drive down. He'd promised CC rides between these legs, so he'd have company he wasn't certain he wanted. It all depended on his reception when he went back to the ranch.

It'd been difficult staying in radio silence over the past two weeks, thus giving Skye time to work through issues. And maybe time to miss him? A guy could only hope.

And he did hope…even while a small part of him said that it was going to take her a long time to trust anyone again.

He had time. He was her business partner.

Tyler's flight landed in Butte at 11:30 p.m. He tossed his duffel into the back of his truck, paid the parking ransom and started driving to Gavin. His plan was simple—get some sleep and whenever Skye was available, they'd discuss the ranch—the safe topic. The last thing he expected was for the lights in her house to be blazing when he drove down the long driveway in the early hours of the morning. When he parked, he saw her pull the curtain back and then drop it again.

Let it be.

He headed past her house and around the bunkhouse to his trailer, stopping when he heard the distinctive sound of her screen door shutting and her footsteps on the porch. Turning back around, he met her at the corner of the bunkhouse.

"I didn't expect you back," she said in a low voice. "Not yet anyway."

"I wanted to drive to Denver."

"Ah." She hugged her arms around herself.

"What are you doing up so late?"

For a moment he thought she wasn't going to answer, but since it was past 2:00 a.m. and she was still fully dressed, she must have figured she had to give some kind of explanation. "I was cleaning."

"Why?"

"It's what I do when I can't sleep."

His lips parted, and he wanted to reach for her. Pull her into his arms and make everything all right—or as right as he could. Skye read his face, took a step back, hugging her arms around herself more tightly.

"How long are you home?"

"I take off on Wednesday." The day after tomorrow. "Is everything okay here?"

"Yeah. Good. I got the chicken house built."

"Can't wait to see it." He hesitated, the duffel growing heavier in his hand. "Can we talk tomorrow before I have to go?"

She let out a soft sigh. "I'm off tomorrow. We can talk. About the ranch."

He glanced up at the starry sky. Things were no better than when he'd left. Maybe now that she'd had time to stew, they were even worse. "Understood."

She turned, but before she made it around the corner, he said, "I am not the enemy, Skye."

He had no idea whether she'd heard him or not.

SKYE AWOKE TO a buzzing text message. Feeling as if she'd gotten a whopping thirty seconds of sleep, she grabbed her phone, noted the time to be 10:30 a.m. and then flopped back against the pillows, bringing the phone with her to read the text. She sat up a little when she saw that it was from Tyler.

Have to take off early for unexpected promo event.

Maybe she had heard a knocking on her door a while back. She thought for a moment, then texted back.

Meet in half an hour?

Sure.

Skye threw back the covers and went to the bathroom to start the shower, then headed to the kitchen to make a new pot of coffee. The one that had been simmering since five thirty, her normal wake-up time, would probably not be all that drinkable. She checked the clock again before she went back to the bathroom. When was the last time she'd overslept?

She showered quickly, dried her hair, then twisted it into a knot on the back of her head before dressing in jeans and an oversize baseball jersey. No one could accuse her of trying to look attractive today, but when she answered the knock on her door ten minutes later, she could see that it didn't matter what she wore. Tyler's gaze zeroed in on her face.

"When do you have to leave?" she asked.

"In about an hour. It's for a local television appearance in Denver. I'm getting interviewed before the event."

"Ah." Skye poured coffee and set two cups on the table, but neither of them sat down. It became obvious after a few seconds that she needn't have poured. She folded her arms and leaned back against the counter. "You did well, I see."

"So far so good."

"The shoulder is holding up?"

He nodded. "I miss you, Skye."

She pressed her fingers against her forehead. "I miss what I thought was true." Her entire foundation had been rocked, and at this point, she didn't know if she had enough foundation left to rebuild. She was hurting. She was numb. And so not ready to slip back into what she and Tyler had started to explore.

"What do you want, Skye?"

She gave a short humorless laugh. "Honestly? To have my ranch back. My life back."

"I wish I could do that for you," Tyler said, getting to his feet. "Unfortunately, I have too much money sunk into the place."

"I know."

She spoke without looking at him. He said nothing and when she glanced up, she found him studying her with a faint frown, and for a moment it was all she could do to breathe correctly.

"Hiding from life isn't going to help, Skye. It's only going to make things worse."

Her chin lifted. "I'm not hiding from life. I'm living it on my terms."

An expression of disbelief combined with something that looked like pity crossed his handsome face, which in turn sparked anger deep inside her. Before she could speak, he said, "I am not Mason."

"I need time, Tyler."

"And you, more than most, should know that time is not guaranteed." He looked as if he wanted to say more, then instead he turned and strode out the door, letting the screen bang shut behind him.

Skye didn't move. She barely breathed.

This was for the best. Tyler could live his life and she could live hers. They might have some awkward moments on the ranch, but it appeared that she'd finally gotten it through his thick bull rider skull that she wouldn't risk getting smacked down again. Not for a long, long time.

WHAT DID IT say about Skye's life that her only confidant was a cat?

It said that she'd gotten exactly what she'd asked for.

At least Skye could vent to Jinx and he wouldn't spill her secrets. Chloe very much wanted Skye to spill her secrets. She didn't know what was wrong, but, because Skye had been unable to hide the fact that *something* was wrong, Chloe was clucking around her like a mama hen. If Angie had still worked there, then Chloe and the world would have known everything, but Cody must have come down hard on his girlfriend, because not one person seemed to know what had transpired between her and Tyler and her dead husband. And Sara Sullivan, the temporary new hire, pretty much kept to herself. She was dealing with an upcoming wedding and an overbearing mother, and it appeared that she had enough issues in her life without concerning herself with those in Skye's life.

"You're worried about your bull rider, aren't you?" Chloe asked seven days after Tyler had left for the second time, and somehow Skye refrained from telling her that Tyler was not *her* bull rider.

"He's a professional and good at what he does," Skye replied evenly. Then, to keep Chloe from continuing to question her, she said, "But of course I worry." She did, and Tyler's comment about not knowing how much time one had didn't help matters.

Chloe seemed happy to have a verified reason for Skye's preoccupation, and Skye was glad she didn't have to explain further how her life had been turned upside down and why. Upside down and inside out. It didn't seem fair that she kept getting hit by stuff, but what could she do except buckle down and deal with matters?

In the week that Tyler had been gone, she had finished her chicken yard and painted the chicken house bright red with white trim. Cliff had some laying hens he was willing to part with, and Skye planned to stop by his place on her first day off. Chickens would make the ranch cheerier, give her something new to focus on. Something to keep her from thinking about the big hole in her life.

She'd felt much the same after Mason died, and, in a way, it was as if he'd died again. How long was it going to take her to get over the fact that he betrayed her in ways she hadn't suspected?

Had there been clues?

She couldn't remember any, but she hadn't been looking. And every time she tried to think of reasons why her husband would stray while on the road, the knife in her heart twisted just a little more. She wanted to rage at Mason. To verbally beat on him. To tell him how he'd destroyed everything that had been good about their relationship with his lies. That she could have forgiven him the gambling, the lies of omission... but not cheating.

She couldn't forgive him, couldn't forgive herself for being so patently unaware.

It was too bad that Tyler was caught in the cross fire, but their relationship had been young. He'd said he loved her. Had practically shaken while he'd said the words, but all they'd done was freeze her up. Mason had professed to love her and she'd believed him, because she wanted to.

She wanted to believe that Tyler loved her, too—and maybe he did. But she was too afraid to believe it. To trust him…or herself.

Tyler did not contact her after leaving. She knew about his rides because she looked them up on the bull-riding sites. He was doing well in the standings, although it would be nip and tuck as to whether he'd make finals after his hiatus. Regardless, he was in the money, which made her feel good. He would be solely dependent on the ranch to see him through the winter financially. Maybe if he earned enough, he'd become an absentee partner. Surely that would be better than the two of them bumping into each other over the course of their days.

And what if he got a girlfriend?

No matter what she told herself, that wouldn't be easy to handle.

Tough. You will handle it.

Skye was getting ready to drive to Cliff's farm when she heard the sound of an engine and looked out her bedroom window to see a familiar truck park next to her car.

Skye's stomach lurched, and she instantly headed for the door. Why would Jess be there unless something had happened to his twin?

"Hey," he called easily as she walked out onto the porch, and her hammering heart slowed.

"Hi." She stopped at the newel post and set a hand on it, hoping she looked calmer than she felt. "What are you doing here?"

"Checking in on my brother's investment."

She frowned. "How so?"

He stopped at the bottom of the stairs, propped his hands on his hips. "I drove to Billings to watch Tyler ride last night, and he asked me to stop by."

And a small part of her had secretly hoped that since he was so close, that he would spend a night or two on the ranch—a very small part that was quickly beaten into submission.

"To check on me or the property?"

"He was pretty clear about it being just the property. He wanted me to have a sit-down with you. Make sure everything is all right, because he probably won't be back for months."

Skye's heart did a double beat. Months. That was what she wanted. Right? Time to recover, get her footing back.

"I didn't see that coming," she said, gesturing for Jess to follow her into the house.

"Neither did I," Jess said as he closed the door behind him. "Tyler always comes home when he's close." He gave Skye a look that she couldn't say she felt comfortable with—as if she were to blame. A second later she decided that she'd misinterpreted, because he smiled at her and asked if she had any coffee left.

After pouring two cups, she sat at the table and Jess sat on the opposite side. "Have you bought hay?"

"I need Tyler's half of the money if we're going to go without a loan this year."

Jess pulled a notebook out of his shirt pocket and jotted down a few words, then looked back up at her. "When are you shipping cows?"

"Two weeks." She cupped her hands around the heavy coffee mug. "Will Tyler be back for that?"

"I don't see that happening. He wants Blaine and me to help you."

"I see." But she didn't. What was with the rock-in-the-pit-of-her-stomach feeling? She forced the corners of her mouth up.

Jess flipped the notebook page. "Tyler wants to buy a few registered Angus to replace the empty cows you're shipping."

"Maybe he and I should talk about that."

Jess looked over the notebook. "As I understand it, talking isn't going that well between you two."

"He told you?"

He smirked at her. "I know my brother."

And what did she say to that?

He closed the notebook. "You know I love you, Skye." When he said it, it didn't feel threatening at all. "But you're ruining my brother."

She was ruining *him*? Right.

Jess reached across the table and pried her hand off her coffee cup, gripping her fingers hard. "My brother has been in love with you forever."

Skye started shaking her head before she was even aware of moving. "I can't help that."

"Yeah?" Jess sounded unimpressed with her adamant tone. "I think you could, if you had the guts."

"Guts?" Skye pulled her fingers out of Jess's grip

and clasped her hands together tightly. "How dare you?" She asked the question flatly, grimly, with no hint of dramatics.

"I dare because I care about both of you."

"That doesn't make things any easier."

He put his hand on top of her clasped hands. "I'm not trying to make things easier for you. I'm looking out for my brother."

Her chin jerked up and she met his gaze. "Did you know about Mason? Not the gambling, but…"

Jess gave a slow nod.

"For how long have you known?"

"Probably since it started." Jess's mouth hardened. "Tyler was so damned angry when he found out." He rubbed his forehead, as if somehow feeling his brother's pain, then set his palm flat on the table. "There was nothing he could do about it."

"He could have told me," she snapped.

Jess leaned forward. "When, Skye? Before Mason died? After? When could he have told you? How would you have taken it?"

Instead of answering, Skye dropped her gaze to her tightly clenched hands, closed her eyes, attempted to gather her thoughts so that she could battle on. She'd been over the same questions a couple hundred times, and there were no easy answers.

"Skye?" Jess's voice softened as he spoke, as if he recognized that she was on the edge of breaking. She wasn't, and she needed to tell him that…but she didn't.

Instead she raised her eyes and said, "This is a complicated matter, Jess."

Complicated and messy and hurtful. She hated being duped and feeling like a fool. She hated that people had known things—bad things—about her husband that she hadn't known.

And…she hated that she totally understood why no one had told her about Mason's behavior.

As much as she wanted to lash out and blame someone, there was no one to blame except for Mason for cheating and herself for not picking up on it—and for blindly trusting her untrustworthy husband.

Where did that leave her?

It left her afraid to trust her own judgment. And she certainly didn't trust those close to her to let her in on secrets that impacted her life in a big way. Angie had known about Mason before she had, and that was simply wrong.

"I agree," Jess said. "It is complicated. But it doesn't need to be impossible." The understanding note in his voice brought her closer to breaking than his accusatory tone had.

Skye swallowed, drew in a breath. Confessed. "I'm afraid."

"I know."

"I thought Mason and I had a good marriage. I could forgive the gambling. But the other… I didn't have a good marriage." Jess nodded and squeezed her hand. "But I thought I did. That's what scares me to death."

"Legitimately so." He cleared his throat. "I know you've been blindsided and I know you have to work through things, but…"

She pressed her lips together, then let loose with the truth. "I've been applying for bank loans again. To buy Tyler out. Things can't continue like they are. It will make us both miserable." Jess scowled at her and Skye frowned back. "It's what I have to do."

"And if you can't get a loan?"

"Then I guess we continue like this, with you as the go-between, until I do get a loan. You said yourself that Tyler didn't want to see me."

"He's doing that for you."

"And I appreciate it."

Jess pushed his untouched coffee aside and got to his feet. "Can you answer me one question?"

"It's probably not a question I want to answer," she said. "But I'll do my best."

"Do you love my brother?"

"It's not a question of love, Jess. It's a question of trust."

"You didn't answer my question."

No she hadn't. And that, in itself, was an answer.

After a few beats of silence, Jess shook his head. "I'll pass the information on to Tyler."

"Thank you."

He went to the door, opened it, then turned back. "One more thing, Skye…"

"What's that?" Her stomach tightened.

"I want you to think—really think—about what you're sacrificing…and what you're gaining."

"And what I'm losing?" she asked lightly, playing the game, thinking that it was so easy to give advice when one's own future and emotions were not involved.

"Yeah."

Chapter Fifteen

Skye hadn't seen Angie since the Founders Day celebration when her world had been turned upside down,
and she assumed that was no accident, since it was
common knowledge that Angie traveled to Gavin on
the weekends to stay with Cody. Therefore, it came as
a surprise to see the former waitress sitting in a booth
on her side of the café early Thursday morning. Skye
picked up her coffeepot and headed over to the table.

"How are you doing?" Angie asked in a subdued
voice as Skye poured the coffee.

"I'm doing okay." Most of the time anyway. Nor-
mally she enjoyed her job, and she was good at it. Today
she wasn't enjoying it so much. An out-of-town couple
had been rude and demanding, and now Angie was here
and Skye had to remind herself that the woman's only
crime, other than partaking in rampant gossip, was
whispering too loudly. "How's cosmetology school?"

"I like it. I think I'll be good at it."

"And think of how much gossip you'll pick up,"
Skye murmured. She was done tiptoeing around people's feelings.

"About that… I'm sorry I was the one who made
you realize that—"

"My husband had cheated on me? I'm better off knowing." Skye held the coffeepot close to her chest. "Don't you think?"

"Cody dumped me after that."

"I didn't know."

"We're back together again...but he made me see some things I hadn't realized before. Like..."

"Gossip hurts?"

Angie pressed her lips together and nodded. Skye gave a casual shrug. "It hurt me, but I'm thankful that I know the whole truth now. So maybe in this case, gossip was a good thing."

"If you say so."

Skye bit her lip and then, after scanning the room to make certain all of her tables were doing okay, slid into the booth across from Angie. "I do say so, and no hard feelings, okay?"

Angie's eyes were getting red. "Cody told me that I'm the reason you and Tyler broke up."

Skye shook her head. "Circumstances did that. I'm..." What? "...not ready for a relationship."

Only a partial truth, that. She'd been ready to ease forward slowly. Tyler had been good with not rushing matters, and then...bam! The truth had smacked her in the face. Scared her back into her hidey-hole.

"I needed to know the truth," she said firmly. "I may not have wanted to know it, but I'm better off." Unless there were other lies out there, but she was fairly certain that her late husband held no more secrets.

Angie reached across the table and touched her hand. "I'm not trying to gossip here, but I think you and Tyler were a good couple and I think you should know that Paige is still following him around."

"Following him?"

"She's been traveling to bull-riding events. Casper. Billings. I've seen her."

Skye sat back against the booth cushions, surprised at how much she hated the idea of Paige being anywhere near Tyler.

"Is that gossip?" Angie asked in a low voice, as if afraid that Cody might find out she'd been telling tales out of school again.

Skye shook her head. "No. It's just the truth, and if she's not keeping things secret, then there's no need for you to do so."

Angie's face brightened. "Yeah. I guess that's the way to measure things."

Skye reached out to pat Angie's arm, then slid out of the booth and picked up the coffeepot. "I agree. The truth isn't gossip, unless there's a reason to keep it secret. Then it's not your place, or mine, to tell the tale."

Angie finished her coffee, then came to the counter to pay and say goodbye. "I hope things are better between us," she said.

Skye gave her a quick hug. "Things are fine. Come see me next time you're in town."

Angie was smiling when she left the café. Skye, not so much.

Paige was following Tyler around?

Well, that had to stop…even though it wasn't really her business. Was it?

It sure felt like her business. Skye glanced around the dining room. Everyone was happily engaged in their meals, so she slipped back to the pantry, propped hands on a shelf and dropped her chin to her chest.

She had no right to be jealous of Paige, but she was.

She wanted Tyler, but she was of terrified of losing again, terrified of trusting and being emotionally back-handed. So freaking scared that she was willing to give up the possibility of happiness for the safety that came of hiding from life.

So what was she going to do about it?

Or better still, what *could* she do about it?

"Excuse me...?"

Skye's head jerked up at the customer's voice and she quickly stepped out of the pantry and headed across the café to her patron. Real life called.

DESPITE HIS SHOULDER INJURY, Tyler was on a roll. He made the semifinals in Denver, the final round in Casper and had won Billings. Even if his shoulder had slid in and out of the socket during the ride, he had every intention of winning again in Spokane. Injury was not an option. He needed the sheer physicality of riding to help battle the frustrations in his life. As long as he was focused on the bull, he was fine. It was during the long drives and the social functions associated with the events that the frustrations built and he found himself getting antsy.

Jess phoned while he was on the road to Spokane with his friend CC sleeping in the passenger seat, head bobbing against the window. Everything was fine on the ranch. No set date for shipping cows, and, well... Skye was looking for financing to buy him out.

That stung.

If he'd done her wrong, if he'd messed up like Mason, or if they'd dated and she'd decided he wasn't her type, he could have lived with it. But that wasn't how it was. He was collateral damage in Skye's battle with fear of loss. She hadn't come out and told him that, but it was too big to miss.

As he saw it, he had two choices—fight back, or walk away gracefully. Give her what she wanted.

"She's doing all right," Jess said. "In a walled-off way...the way she was after Mason died."

Because she was mourning another loss. This one probably almost as devastating as the first. Now she didn't even have fond memories. She had nothing.

Ty had a strong feeling that she also wanted nothing, except to maybe be left alone.

"You won't be making Spokane, will you?"

"Wish I could. I have to be in Kalispell the next day." A short silence hung between them, and then Jess said, "If you want to move your trailer onto my lot, there's room."

"Yeah. I know." He'd already done his figuring there, and now, once again, his question was should he stay on the ranch he owned part of, move to his brother's place or maybe head down to Texas, where, even if he couldn't put Skye out of his head, he could at least put some distance between them?

The one thing he did know was that he needed to dissolve their partnership, so that if he and Skye ever did try to hash things out between them, there wouldn't be a ranch hanging between them.

THERE WERE FRESH tire tracks on her driveway when Skye drove in but no vehicle and no sign of a package delivery. Someone needing directions, perhaps?

No. It had been Tyler, there and gone while she'd been at work. He'd left a note on her locked front door telling her that he'd left something for her in his trailer.

Skye folded the note and carried it with her as she retraced her steps down the path and around the bunkhouse to the trailer. It was unlocked, so she opened the door and stepped inside.

It smelled like Tyler.

She pressed her lips together after inhaling deeply, then crossed to the table where a large envelope with her name on it lay. She opened it and pulled out the single sheet of paper.

The mortgage agreement. At the bottom he had printed PAID IN FULL.

What the heck?

Skye sank down on the hard cushion of the futon-like sofa. There was only one reason he would have done this. He was leaving. Going to Texas as he'd once said he was. In fact, there was a Texas road map lying on top of a stack of books.

Skye closed her eyes, feeling ridiculously close to tears. Things were happening too quickly. Yes, she'd thought she wanted to end things before they became too serious, but now she feared they already were too serious.

She felt like her stomach was turning inside out. *I love him...and I'm a coward. I'm using Mason's betrayal as an excuse to hide from the normal risks one takes in life.*

What was it Tyler had said to her? You never know how much time you have. Skye put the agreement back into the envelope and slid in the note Tyler had left on her front door.

Then she reached into her pocket for her phone, pulled up her contact list, drew in a deep breath and yet again prepared to eat humble pie. When the line picked up, she said, "Hello, Jess...I need a favor."

THE LAST TIME Skye had been in Nampa, Idaho, had been with Mason, just after they were married. She'd traveled to several events with her new husband before settling in to run the ranch and earn their one steady paycheck by working at the café. Skye hadn't loved living alone for weeks at a time, but it wasn't something she hated, either. It was the reality of their existence, and she knew it would last for only a matter of years before Mason retired from bull riding and ranched full-time.

Little had she known...

But Skye wasn't going there. Yes, she was borderline terrified, but letting the past color her future to the extent that she embraced the idea of rattling around in an empty life because it was "safe" bordered on wrong. And cowardly.

Face the truth.

Her seat was not the best, but what could she expect for minimum dollar and last minute? She was squeezed between a family with four children happily eating gooey cotton candy and an elderly couple wearing very large cowboy hats. Twice Skye had cotton candy stuck in her hair before the child's mother intervened and changed seats with her daughter.

"Sorry," she murmured.

"Not a problem." Skye sat up straighter as the show began. The arena lights dimmed, smoke swirled and the bull riders walked out into the arena as colored LED lights danced over them. She instantly recognized Tyler by his walk, and her heart swelled.

She was not giving this guy up.

She only hoped that giving up the ranch didn't mean that he was giving up on her. He was a bull rider. Stubborn.

Then the lights went low and the show began. Skye dodged another wallop from the cotton candy as the little girl squeezed past her to head for the restroom with her mother, then settled in to watch her guy do what he loved.

She didn't have long to wait. Tyler was up fourth, and after the usual fanfare, the gateman pulled the rope and Little Biscuit, a big Charolais-Brahman cross, exploded out of the chute and she realized that, just as he'd once promised, he was wearing a helmet. No more stitched-up face. Not unless he got clocked really good.

Little Biscuit spun to his left then flipped his hind end the opposite direction, throwing Tyler over his hand. He pushed deep, recovered and was well settled by the time Little Biscuit did his opposite spin. Four seconds left. Three…

The bull did a high buck and looked as if he was going to sunfish, but instead came down with a jarring front-end landing as the buzzer rang. A cheer went up from the crowd, but Skye stayed where she was, gripping the seat on either side of her until Tyler disembarked and rolled as the bull bucked past him toward the gate.

Only then did she lean back and let out the breath she'd been holding for fifteen long seconds.

HE WAS A winner and a loser. Tyler hadn't taken home the top check, but he'd scored third, and that made him a winner. Walking out of the arena alive made him a winner. It was having no one and nowhere to go home to that gave him the loser feeling.

He'd have to see about moving his trailer off the property. His parents had assured him they'd love to see him in Texas. He imagined they would.

Problem was…he was a Montana guy, and it was hard to change that.

He'd been interviewed, along with several other riders, immediately following the event, and then he'd had to get his shoulder bandaged up to immobilize it—just a precaution, since once again it had felt as if it had slid in and out of the socket.

Just a few more months…like four. He could do this.

He left the arena by a side door, stepping into an almost empty parking lot. The next event was on the other side of the Mississippi, and he was flying. He'd park his truck at Jess's, see what he could do about his current living situation. His boots echoed on the pavement, and as he approached his truck, he slowed.

Maybe he'd been hit in the head harder than he'd realized when he'd gone to the ground, because the woman leaning against his truck, head down, hugging her arms around herself, looked just like Skye, about five hundred miles from where she was supposed to be. As he started walking faster, and his footsteps began echoing on the pavement, her head snapped up, and his heart tumbled.

"Skye?"

She stepped away from the truck, and then her spine stiffened as she took in his bandaged arm. "Is it bad?" she asked.

"Depends." He stopped a goodly distance away from her. If she was here, that was good. But his gut told him to move slowly. Find out the whole story. "Did you get my note?"

"I did."

"And?"

She took a couple of steps toward him, arms still crossed over her body as if she were protecting herself. But when she stopped in front of him, she dropped her arms to her sides and tilted up her chin. "Thank you for the gift, but I don't want it."

"That makes no sense at all."

"It does if I want to keep you around."

His heart did a couple of hard beats against his ribs. He turned his head to look at her sideways. "You better take this offer while you can." The fair-play part of him insisted that he say those words. "I may be bankrupt by this time next year."

She shook her head.

"Why do you want to keep a broken-down bull rider around?"

"I love him."

Another double beat of his heart. Tyler wanted to move closer but instead stayed put. No more jumping ahead of himself, buying ranches and the like. "Do you trust him?"

"Yes," she said simply. "If I don't have trust, then I have a ranch house with just me and a cat in it. Which was fine a couple of months ago, but it's not fine anymore." She exhaled, and it sounded shaky, as if her voice was on the edge of breaking. "I need you, Tyler."

That was when he moved, ignoring the pain as he pulled her against him, found her lips. Every time he kissed the woman it felt like a homecoming, and it was no different tonight.

"So," he murmured against her lips, "you want to keep things as they are?"

"Yes. As they are. We're partners." She eased back a little, so that they could see each other clearly.

"Let me make certain I totally understand." Because he wanted this carved in stone. "You want to be with me."

"Yes."

His eyes narrowed as he thought of Annie and Trace and Lex and Grady.

"Maybe you could travel with me?"

She brought her hands back up to frame his face. "Maybe...but I have chickens in addition to my job. It's a big responsibility."

"Jess has often expressed a deep interest in chickens."

"Funny thing—that's kind of what he's doing now. Watching my new chickens."

"You're kidding."

"His trailer had plumbing issues, and I'm letting him stay in the house." She let her hands slide down to the front of his chest. "I wanted to watch you ride. I never have, you know. I only knew you by reputation."

"What did you think?"

"It stirred my blood."

Tyler laughed even as he continued to grapple with the fact that Skye was here. She wanted him. She trusted him. "I can think of other ways to stir your blood."

"I know...and don't think I don't love that about you. I just need one promise from you."

"Name it."

"I need the truth. No matter what. If I know the truth, then I'm dealing with reality. Not illusions and not fears. Can you do that for me? Even when it's hard?"

He kissed her so gently and tenderly, his palm caressing her cheek as he made his promise to her. "Yes. I will always tell you the truth. You can depend on me."

* * * * *

*Be sure to check out the
other books in Jeannie Watt's*
MONTANA BULL RIDERS *miniseries,*
THE BULL RIDER MEETS HIS MATCH
and
THE BULL RIDER'S HOMECOMING,
available now from Harlequin Western Romance.

And look for a new MONTANA BULL RIDERS *story
coming soon, wherever Harlequin books are sold!*

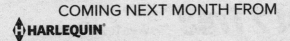
#1641 THE COWBOY UPSTAIRS
Cupid's Bow, Texas • by Tanya Michaels
Becca Johnston is raising her son alone, and Sawyer McCall, the hot cowboy renting a room in her house, is a distraction she doesn't need. But she can't deny she wants him to stay.

#1642 MADE FOR THE RANCHER
Sapphire Mountain Cowboys • by Rebecca Winters
When Wymon Clayton rescues a woman after a small-plane crash, he has no idea that Jasmine Telford—beautiful, sophisticated, worldly—is destined to be the wife of a simple rancher. Him!

#1643 THE RANCHER'S BABY PROPOSAL
The Hitching Post Hotel • by Barbara White Daille
When Reagan Chase returns to his hometown, Ally Marinez is thrilled to find her high school crush now wants her—as a nanny for his newborn son! She accepts, determined to be the woman of his dreams.

#1644 THE COWBOY'S ACCIDENTAL BABY
Cowboys of Stampede, Texas • by Marin Thomas
Lydia Canter has always wanted a family, but she never imagined the father of her baby being bull rider Gunner Hardell. This good-time cowboy has to prove he can be the kind of man she needs!

Becca Johnston doesn't need a distraction like her new tenant, rugged rodeo champ Sawyer McCall. But having a good man around the house means so much to her young son and she's definitely enjoying the handsome cowboy's attention...

Read on for a sneak preview of
THE COWBOY UPSTAIRS,
the next book in Tanya Michaels's
CUPID'S BOW, TEXAS series.

"Mr. Sawyer, do you like pizza?"

"As a matter of fact, I love it."

"Then you should—"

"Marc! Scoot."

"—have dinner with us."

Becca bit back a groan.

"Well," he said as the door clattered shut, "at least one of you likes me."

Now that he was on the step just below her, she could see his eyes were green, flecked with gold, and she hated herself for noticing. "So is Sawyer your first name or last?"

"First. Sawyer McCall." He extended a hand. "Pleasure to meet you. Officially."

Her fingers brushed over his in something too brief to qualify as a handshake before she pulled away. "Becca Johnston. What are you doing here?"

"I need a place to stay."

She bit the inside of her lip. When she'd had the bright idea to rent out her attic, she certainly hadn't considered giving the key to a smug, sexy stranger.

"I can pay up front. Cash. And I can give you a list of references to assure you I'm not some whack job."

"Mr. McCall, I really don't think—"

The screen door banged open and a mini tornado gusted across the porch in the form of her son. "You're still here! Are you staying for pizza? Mama, can I show him my space cowboys and robot horses?"

Becca studied her son's eager face and tried to recall the last time she'd seen him look so purely happy. "Mr. McCall and I aren't finished talking yet, champ. Why don't you go set the table for three?"

Marc disappeared back inside as quickly as he'd come.

She took a deep breath. "The attic apartment has its own back stair entrance and a private bathroom. Whoever I rent the room to is welcome to join Marc and I for meals—but, in exchange, I was hoping to find someone with a bit of child-care experience. Occasional babysitting in trade for my cooking."

He shrugged. "Sounds reasonable."

"Then, assuming your references check out, you've got a deal, Mr. McCall."

His grin, boldly triumphant and male, sent tiny shivers up her arms. "When do I get to see my room?"

Don't miss THE COWBOY UPSTAIRS
by Tanya Michaels, available May 2017 wherever
Harlequin® Western Romance
books and ebooks are sold.

www.Harlequin.com

Turn your love of reading into rewards you'll love with

Harlequin My Rewards

**Join for FREE today at
www.HarlequinMyRewards.com**

Earn **FREE BOOKS** of your choice.

Experience **EXCLUSIVE OFFERS** and contests.

Enjoy **BOOK RECOMMENDATIONS**
selected just for you.

PLUS! Sign up now
and get **500** points
right away!

HARLEQUIN®

A *Romance* FOR EVERY MOOD™

Love the Harlequin book you just read?

Your opinion matters.

Review this book on your favorite
book site, review site, blog or your own
social media properties and share
your opinion with other readers!